"How come you never told me about her?"

"What?" Sara glared at Kirk. She'd spent months hating him for rejecting his daughter, and now he claimed that he'd never known about Abby? "I wrote you about Abby twice."

"I didn't get anything about Abby."

"When you didn't answer—"

"I didn't get them," he insisted in a voice that reminded her of a soft sheath housing the sharpest of blades. He hesitated. "And I want to know my daughter."

"She's *our* daughter."

"I missed you, Sara. I was hoping you would give us another chance."

He looked so sincere, as if he believed it. But she couldn't allow herself to hope. "I can't."

Dear Reader,

HEROES INC. is my brand-new Harlequin Intrigue series about the highly trained men hired by legendary ex-CIA agent Logan Kincaid to take on the most impossible of missions. Okay, think irresistibly sexy heroes. Think of a team of men with hard heads, skilled hands and soft hearts.

I've always enjoyed reading books that could sweep me away into a world of adventure. Writing them is no different. And this book kicks off the trilogy with a grand adventure that will have you sitting on the edge of your seat. I came up with the idea for *Daddy to the Rescue* while watching the television show *Survivor*. I kept thinking about where the producers put the show—always in warm places—and I thought, how would a woman survive in the cold? Alone with a baby? With no food or matches?

So I stranded Sara Hardaker in the Rocky Mountains during a blizzard. But of course, I had to send a handsome hero to the rescue, who just so happens to be her ex-husband. However, in the end, I'm not really sure who saved whom.

I enjoy hearing from readers, so please feel free to stop by my Web site: www.SusanKearney.com. Happy reading!

Susan Kearney

DADDY TO THE RESCUE
SUSAN KEARNEY

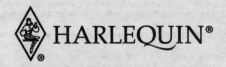

TORONTO • NEW YORK • LONDON
AMSTERDAM • PARIS • SYDNEY • HAMBURG
STOCKHOLM • ATHENS • TOKYO • MILAN • MADRID
PRAGUE • WARSAW • BUDAPEST • AUCKLAND

ISBN 0-373-22705-1

DADDY TO THE RESCUE

Visit us at www.eHarlequin.com

Printed in U.S.A.

ABOUT THE AUTHOR

Susan Kearney used to set herself on fire four times a day. Now she does something really hot—she writes romantic suspense. While she no longer performs her signature fire dive (she's taken up figure skating), she never runs out of ideas for characters and plots. A business graduate from the University of Michigan, Susan is working on her next novel and writes full-time. She resides in a small town outside Tampa, Florida, with her husband and children and a spoiled Boston terrier. Visit her at http://www.SusanKearney.com.

Books by Susan Kearney

HARLEQUIN INTRIGUE

*The Sutton Babies
†Hide and Seek
**The Crown Affair
††Heroes, Inc.

Don't miss any of our special offers. Write to us at the following address for information on our newest releases.

Harlequin Reader Service
U.S.: 3010 Walden Ave., P.O. Box 1325, Buffalo, NY 14269
Canadian: P.O. Box 609, Fort Erie, Ont. L2A 5X3

CLASSIFIED

For Your Information.
Read and Destroy.

The SHEY GROUP is a private paramilitary organization whose purpose is to take on high-risk, high-stakes missions in accord with U.S. government policy. All members are former CIA, FBI or military with top-level clearances and specialized skills. Members maintain close ties to the intelligence community and conduct high-level behind-the-scenes operations for the government as well as for private individuals and corporations.

The U.S. government will deny any connection with this group.

Employ at your own risk.

CAST OF CHARACTERS

Kirk Hardaker—The canine specialist and Shey Group operative has been assigned his toughest mission of all: to find his missing ex-wife…and the child he's never met.

Sara Hardaker—The genius behind the latest in face-recognition software, she's set on living her life as a single mother.

Abby Hardaker—Sara has kept her eight-month-old daughter a secret from her ex-husband, until now.…

Logan Kincaid—Legendary founder of the Shey Group, the ex-CIA agent handpicked Kirk for this latest covert mission.

Ryker Stevens—Ex-Special Forces with an MBA, Ryker's specialty is cracking financial codes, but can he use it to help Kirk?

Garth Davis—Sara's friendly competitor? Or ruthless thief?

"The Cowboy"—The eccentric millionaire knows Sara's software could make him an even richer man.

For Patricia Smith, an editor whose wise guidance
is much appreciated. Thanks, Patricia!

Prologue

Trying and failing to relax, Sara Hardaker stared out the window of the private jet the government had sent to fly her to her meeting. As the only passenger on the plane besides her daughter, Abby, she had a prime window to look out at the crisp blue sky and admire the wisps of clouds as fine as Abby's silky blond hair.

Awake in the seat beside her, at eight months, Abby was a great traveler. Although she didn't like her confinement in her car seat, the monotonous thrum of the private jet's engines would soon soothe the baby to sleep. She'd already breast-fed, and since they were the only passengers, they'd had plenty of privacy.

Sara hadn't seen the pilot since she'd strapped herself into her seat. The small plane had no copilot and no flight attendants. But Sara counted herself lucky that the government considered her work important enough that it would arrange such luxurious private transportation. She could get used to traveling in plush leather seats with a fully stocked kitchen and bar at her disposal. After she completed the sale of her software to the government, she and Abby would be able to afford to take a nice vacation to someplace warm and sunny.

Months of hard work were about to pay off. Several government agencies were impressed with Sara's face-recognition software, and she thanked her lucky stars that she'd had the courage to leave the corporate world to become an entrepreneur. Her company might be small and consist of only one person, but she'd succeeded in writing the computer code that could identify faces from a digitalized picture, even if a terrorist wore sunglasses and a hat, even in bad light.

"Ball." Practiced in gaining her mother's attention, Abby tossed a plastic ball at Sara. The toy landed in her lap. Sara grinned and handed the ball back to Abby, knowing her daughter would simply repeat the maneuver. Sara didn't mind. Abby was the one person who could draw her from thoughts about work. Her daughter had started to speak at an unusually early age.

Sara was tempted to teach Abby more words but Abby really needed to sleep, not play. Sara stroked her baby's neck in an effort to divert her attention from their game. The trip would go faster if Abby slept. Soon her eyes started to flutter closed.

Abby usually went at full speed until she succumbed to sleep.

But in the airplane Sara couldn't allow her active child to climb out of her seat to crawl and explore. At the best of times, Abby was a handful. Sara considered the baby a blessing, though. Abby kept her anchored firmly in the real world.

Otherwise, Sara tended to lose track of time while she worked in cyberspace. For Abby, she'd given up eighteen-hour days. And for the sake of her daughter's future, she was making this very important trip. But Abby wasn't supposed to have been with her. When the sitter came down with the flu, Sara had had no choice but to bring Abby along.

Sara looked down at her precious daughter, who had fallen into a deep sleep. But even as she dreamed, kicking her tiny feet, the baby held onto her ball. Sara automatically smoothed back Abby's hair and prayed she wouldn't wake until the plane landed in Los Angeles.

Looking down through the clouds, Abby spied the bleak snow-covered peaks and foggy valleys of the Rocky Mountains. Another hour, maybe an hour and a half, until they landed, she estimated.

When the pilot opened the door separating the cabin from the cockpit, Sara realized she must have dozed. Her first glance went to Abby, who was still sleeping soundly.

Sara pulled a loose sock back onto her daughter's foot, then glanced at the pilot. "Who's flying the—"

Oh my God!

The man held her computer briefcase full of books in one hand and opened the door with the other. Wind roared into the plane. She had an image of a back-pack—no…a parachute—on his back. He jumped. With her computer bag.

Leaving them with no pilot. No copilot.

The nose dived, and the plane accelerated. She was crushed into her seat. And all Sara could think about was that Abby wasn't supposed to be here. But she was. They were both going to die. The pilot had obviously wanted her new computer program. Sara glanced at the laptop she'd removed earlier and had slipped into the diaper bag of Abby's car seat. They hadn't succeeded in stealing her program or the specialized hard drive that ran her work, but she got no satisfaction from the thought.

The plane plunged toward the mountains with sickening speed. Within seconds, it would smash into the harsh chaos of trees, ice and rock.

In the bucking, diving plane, Sara reached for and, somehow, found Abby's tiny hand.

Chapter One

Kirk Hardaker liked the cute one with the adorable eyes, the one who knew how to shake her tail, but he needed to check them all out. Only the best would do. One that came easily to him. No bullies. Since temperament was as critical to success as intelligence, he set high standards, requiring all his partners to be playful as well as smart before he'd waste his time on them or offer them a home on his Michigan ranch.

Kirk was in no rush. Developing a strong rapport required patience and years of training, but the reward was often a happy, warm body to snuggle at one's feet after a long day.

With a sharp eye toward behavior that revealed character, Kirk surveyed his choices. The shy pup in the corner wouldn't serve his purposes. Nor would the one ignoring the ball he'd just thrown into the middle of the litter. However, the puppy who'd chased the ball and brought it back to him might work out just fine.

He patted the six-week-old German shepherd on the head, her reward for returning the ball, and was pleased to see that she neither feared him nor snapped at him. Carefully, he lifted the animal out of the pen and placed her in grass that topped her head by a good five inches. When she didn't freeze or whine to return to the litter, but inquisitively headed north, he approvingly watched her explore, stopping occasionally to lift her head and sniff the air.

Kirk removed a knotted rag from his pocket and dropped it in front of the pup. Eagerly, she played tug-of-war, not the least concerned over her unfamiliar surroundings.

So far, so good. He had yet to test the pup to see if she feared loud noises, water, heights or uneven terrain beneath her paws—all such fears unacceptable in a top-notch search and rescue dog. However, the owner of this litter had left the dogs with Kirk for a week, and he had several days left to make his choice.

Kirk needed the leisure to go slowly and choose carefully. He'd spend hundreds of hours training each animal, and so refused to rush his selection process. Out here on his isolated acreage from which a trip to town took half a day, the seasons ruled his working hours. During the long daylight hours of summer, Kirk had worked long and hard at his newly chosen career, determined to train the best search and rescue dogs in the country. Winter would curtail some of his training activities, giving him a chance to catch up on his ever-mounting correspondence. He often read after supper, studying the latest training manuals and poring over catalogues of the latest gear and equipment.

As he scooped up the pup and rewarded her with a good scratch behind the ears, he heard the sound of a helicopter. He looked up and saw an Air Force

MH53J Pave. His dogs in the pens barked ferociously at the loud machine invading their turf. He placed the pup back in the litter and headed toward his cabin.

He didn't get many visitors. It was too soon for the pups' owner to return, and he certainly wouldn't arrive by *helicopter*. Two weeks ago some campers had gotten lost and Kirk had given them directions back to the highway. No one else had been out here for months. It was unlikely, anyway, that a lost tourist had taken a bad turn in a chopper.

While still in the military, he'd sometimes imagined his promotion arriving in a chopper like this one. A high-level officer would exit and offer him the opportunity to oversee worldwide K-9 operations, a job he'd coveted since his days in boot camp. Promotions in his area of expertise came slowly and, although he'd been among the world's best in the field, he'd had to wait for room at the top. Well, he was through waiting. That part of his life was over. Oh, he was still dedicated, but now he worked for himself. He'd leased the land for this ranch to train his dogs, and found the work surprisingly rewarding. Someday he hoped to purchase the acreage. So the men in the chopper overhead had nothing that could persuade him to leave—not even the head position in worldwide operations would tempt him to re-up. But perhaps the landing had nothing to do with him. The chopper might simply be low on fuel or be experiencing engine trouble.

When a tall, dark-haired man in a black leather coat exited the pilot's seat, Kirk stiffened. This man wasn't lost. And he didn't need fuel. From his ramrod-straight back, Kirk pegged the stranger as an officer. High-ranked. Trouble.

Kirk knew the type so well because he had once been one of them. No more. He chose to serve his country in another way now—a way that gave him peace.

Kirk waited for the man to come to him, convinced that no exchange of words would alter his plans. He'd had several offers by phone—calls he hadn't bothered to answer. He wasn't interested in going back. He'd made a new life for himself. A good one.

However, the United States military wasn't the best in the world without reason. They were experts at recruitment. And when they needed his kind of specialized expertise, they had no qualms about asking him to reenlist. Not today, he wouldn't. Not ever again.

The sharp-eyed pilot removed a leather glove and offered his hand. "I'm Logan Kincaid."

Not military. Kirk recognized the man's name. Classified. Probably CIA. The man's reputation was known only by those in the highest government circles. It was rumored that Logan Kincaid had worked with NORAD as well as NASA—his specialty was programming satellite communications—and that he'd written the code for America's secret antimissile defense program. The only reason Kirk had heard about Kincaid was that his ex-wife, Sara, a brilliant programmer in her own right, had had to gain permission to use some of Kincaid's code in her own work.

"And you're with?" Kirk prodded.

"The Shey Group."

Kirk had never heard of the Shey Group. He shook the man's hand, not bothering to speak his own name, which Logan obviously already knew. A man like him didn't fly a chopper four hundred miles north of Detroit without knowing the name of the man he'd come to meet. And if what Kirk suspected was true, Logan Kincaid—the numero-uno computer guru in the United States—had already read his top-secret military file, and knew his credit rating and to the dollar how much he paid for the lease on this land. So what?

When they shook hands, Kincaid didn't flinch at the dirt covering Kirk's fingers and palms.

Kirk pierced the man with a hard stare. "You've wasted your time coming out here. I don't own a computer."

At Kirk's lame joke, Logan's facial expression didn't change. A flicker of respect in his eyes, however, let Kirk know the man hadn't anticipated that Kirk would know anything about his hush-hush world. And Kirk didn't want to know. His stint in the military had already cost him too much.

"If you know who I am, you know I don't usually make house calls."

Sensing that Logan wouldn't leave until he'd been heard out, Kirk gestured toward the cabin with resignation. "Would you like a beer?"

"No, thanks. I didn't come to drink."

"Is this where I'm supposed to ask why you came?" Kirk asked with a shake of his head. "Because your reason doesn't matter to me. I'm not interested in joining or rejoining any government organizations."

"Okay."

"You've wasted some of that very valuable time of yours. You should have phoned."

"I did—"

Logan, seeming a bit amused, followed Kirk into the cabin and removed his long leather coat. He wore a sharp suit and tie that would look ridiculous on another pilot and would have made most men feel out of place. Not Logan Kincaid.

"—You didn't return my call."

Kirk shrugged, walked straight to the kitchen sink and thoroughly washed his hands. The message light on his answering machine was blinking red, and Kirk tried and failed to recall the last time he'd listened to the messages. He dried his hands, giving Logan time to take a good look around his one-room cabin.

Between a kitchen and bathroom that boasted indoor plumbing, thanks to water from a nearby creek, and an electric generator that fueled his stove, kept the lights on and warmed the place if the fireplace fell behind, he had all the comforts he'd required to settle in. However, he wasn't much of a housekeeper. Magazines and books cluttered the deep leather sofa and a mismatched kitchen table and chairs that had been left from the former owners. Unpacked canned goods still tumbled over in their grocery bags. Dog fur clung to his boots like magnets and then tracked onto the floor. And a stack of last month's newspapers and mail lay scattered on the kitchen counters.

"Feel free to clear off a spot and make yourself comfortable."

Logan emptied a chair full of clean but unfolded

laundry, tossed it on the couch and sat. "I no longer work for our government in an official capacity."

"I'm not interested, especially not in a kite operation." Kite operations were the most dangerous assignments. If something went wrong, the government cut the agent free and then denied all knowledge of the operation. During his military stint in Kuwait, Logan and his dog had mostly searched for bombs during routine embassy sweeps. But occasionally, he'd volunteered to go on special missions, where planes flew over borders without permission to places where American soldiers had no legal right to be. Kirk had never sweated the ethics. His job had been simple. Check the premises for bombs so people wouldn't die.

But good people *had* died.

Don't go there.

And then he'd taken other dogs on search and rescue missions. Looking for people who had survived mud slides, gas explosions, bombing raids, train wrecks, and earthquakes was rewarding work. Work he now left for other handlers.

"I'm here because I was hired to do a job."

"Hired?"

"My firm, the Shey Group, is a team of highly trained, mostly ex-military men skilled in the use of weapons, covert ops and hand-to-hand combat. I've come to recruit you—"

"And I'm still not interested."

"Each team member owns stock in the company. We'd be willing to pay you one million dollars—"

"No." The higher the pay, the greater the danger. And he'd promised himself that no matter how urgent the plea, he wouldn't heed the request. As one of the best dog handlers in the world, Kirk's expertise was in high demand. But he could do more good by staying right here and training the animals that were also in high demand. In a year, he could train dozens of dogs, who would go on to save more lives than he would if he kept leaving on missions of mercy.

"One million dollars, for one or two days' work."

Kirk shook his head, not the least bit tempted. He would stay here, perhaps buy the puppy, and continue to train his animals.

"You just turned down more money than you'll probably earn in your lifetime."

"So?"

"So if you'd said yes to the money, you would have been the wrong man for the team."

"I don't understand."

"I only recruit team members who are willing to put their lives on the line for one another. I've found that men motivated by money aren't usually willing to do so."

Kirk shot Logan an appraising look. Slowly he nodded. "Makes sense." He ran a hand through his hair, which needed a good cut. Come to think of it, he'd been so eager to work with the dogs that he hadn't shaved after he'd showered this morning, either. But a man like Logan obviously didn't measure a man by his appearance, although he himself was immaculately groomed. Logan had gone to a lot of trouble to seek him out; the least he could do was set the man up with another skilled handler. First he needed to determine what specialization was needed.

"What kind of mission is it? Drugs? Bomb sniffing?"

"Tracking and protection."

An unusual combination. Dogs were either trained to track or to protect. Not both. And he speculated on what kind of person would first need to be found, then protected. Kirk tried to keep up with the news, but he was often days behind.

"Did some terrorist bust loose from prison?"

"A private plane went down over the Rocky Mountains. We need a search and rescue."

"I'm sure you know people in the protection business. I'll give you the names of some good handlers." Kirk reached for a pad of paper and a pen.

"Don't." Logan stood, his expression fierce. "There are complications."

"There always are. The Rockies have snow that's hip deep. Temperature's bound to be below freezing come nightfall."

"Twenty degrees. Just before the plane went down this morning without warning, an observer on the ground saw a man jump out of the plane and parachute to safety."

Kirk's heart kicked his ribs. "That's murder. Are we talking more terrorism?"

Logan shook his head. "There were only two people on the small private plane. One was your ex-wife."

Oh…my…God. That's why Logan had come to him. All his reasons for refusing just withered and died, and Kirk's mouth turned so dry he could barely speak. This had to be a mistake.

"Sara?"

"And her baby daughter."

A ray of hope shot through him. Government bureaucracies often made errors. "You must be mistaken. Sara doesn't have a daughter."

"Sara named her Abby."

Abby had been Sara's grandmother's name.

Kirk fought past budding panic. Even when Sara had been just a kid herself at age sixteen, she'd already decided to name her first female child after the woman who'd taken her in and raised her when her parents died in a car accident. Sara was always planning years ahead like that. She had schedules for practically everything, from buying a house, to paying off the mortgage, to…having a baby.

Logan gave him only a moment to digest the disastrous news before briefing him further. "We haven't heard any radio messages since the plane went down."

"Sara always carries a cell phone." He looked hopefully at Logan.

"My experts tell me that the mountains could be blocking a signal."

"Have you located the crash site?"

"We've narrowed the possibilities. Search parties are already combing the area, but—" he shrugged "—the terrain is rugged."

And lethal. Even if she'd survived the crash uninjured, even if she was in excellent shape and had good wilderness survival skills, she could freeze on that mountain. And he knew that for all her wonderful qualities, Sara was no athlete and she didn't even like camping. However, she was the most determined woman he'd ever known. He hoped that determination would keep her alive.

Kirk stood, grabbed a pack and shoved in clothing and gear with methodical thoroughness. "How soon can you get me there?"

THE CHOPPER TRIP to the Detroit airport seemed to take forever. Pepper, his best search dog, settled calmly at Kirk's feet. The four-year-old German shepherd, her ears up, appeared more than ready for the mission.

So did Logan, who piloted the chopper as easily as he gave orders. During the trip, he made dozens of phone calls to his team, coordinating their efforts, arranging the transport of men and supplies and equipment to base camp, including flights with the military when necessary—even getting a judge out of bed to authorize a wiretap on a promising lead. Apparently, the team was going after the bastards who'd tried to murder a woman and child.

Physically, Kirk was as prepared for this mission as Logan and Pepper. Handlers kept themselves in triathlon athletic shape. Whether running beside their dogs for hours, swimming across lakes or climbing snow-laden mountains, they had to keep up with their four-legged partners. And in a successful recovery, speed often made the difference between life and death.

Handlers were called in to the world's worst disaster sites, working in areas where machines couldn't go. In the Rockies, just finding the plane crash site was a huge headache. Satellite surveillance was often no help. Snow and trees could hide a downed plane.

So could steep ravines. To make matters worse, the wreckage could be spread out over a very wide area, hindering the search for people or bodies even further.

He refused to consider the possibility that Sara might be dead. Only hope would give him the necessary strength to get through the next minutes, hours and days.

Hang on, Sara. We're coming to get you.

He knew she would try. Sara never gave up. The word *quit* wasn't in her vocabulary. Kirk had learned that very quickly, the first time they'd met.

At sixteen, he'd been a jock. Quarterback of the football team, a mid-distance track star and the school's best five-hundred-yard freestyle swimmer. With some of the sports' seasons overlapping, his grades had slipped and he'd been assigned a tutor.

A load of books under his arm, he'd been whistling when he strode into the study hall. Popular, confident, he assumed this tutor would do all his work for him. At the sight of The Brain, however, his spirits sank. With her blond hair tangled around her face and huge dark glasses, he could barely see her features. But he knew her reputation. She took all honors classes. She would graduate valedictorian. And she had no friends. Rumor was that she spoke only in computer code.

He was pretty sure his athletic ability wouldn't impress her; in fact, he doubted she'd ever attended a sporting event. But she could hardly miss his letter jacket and the bold *M* for Michigan High School emblazoned in white with gray piping.

Most girls would give him shy or come-hither smiles. Both kinds were welcoming.

She didn't look up, but growled, "You're late."

"Does it matter?"

"Of course it matters. We only have an hour a day, three days a week. And you are flunking."

"I'm not failing. I have a *D*." Technically, he was correct. However, the test he'd taken that morning had yet to be averaged in.

She handed him a paper. The test had a giant red *F* on top. She was right. His *D* had just turned to an *F*.

"Take a seat. You'll find we get along better if you don't argue with me."

He didn't like failing. Didn't like the way she spoke to him. But he needed her. His school had a rule that failing athletes couldn't compete in after-school activities—like football. Most of his teachers let him skate by, but the computer teacher wasn't interested in sports either. Kirk had been counting on the tutor doing his homework and bringing up his grade enough to pass.

He held out his hand. "Just give me my finished homework and I'll be gone."

That got her attention. Since he was still standing, she was forced to crane her neck to look up at him. She had braces and those horrible glasses, so telling what she looked like wasn't easy. However, he had always liked to look, really look, at things and people. His ability to notice details had made him not only an excellent athlete, but more perceptive than other kids his age. And he suspected that when the braces came off and when someone convinced her to stop hiding behind those glasses, the ugly duckling would turn into a beauty. She had great bones, full lips and killer hair—if she would only brush it.

"You expect *me* to do your homework?"

He swung his arm and set the books down beside her. "Isn't that why you're here?"

"Hell, no. I'm here because the National Honors Society requires me to spend a number of hours tutoring jocks like you."

"That means you have to help me?"

"That means I teach, you listen. You don't have to like it. I don't have to like it, but I will not only complete the requirement, I will do it well." She poked her finger into his stomach. "And that means teaching you basic HTML."

She sounded fierce and determined, like the football coach before a hard workout. And at the challenge, he grinned. "You think I'm going to pass?"

"When I'm done with you, you're going to have an *A*."

No one had ever spoken to him like The Brain. She made him mad, and just for fun, he teased her. "I never get *A*'s."

"*I've* never been your tutor," she countered with a confidence that made him believe her.

Reeled in by her conviction, he took the seat beside her. She started from scratch and laid out the course work more logically than the teacher had. She didn't make it easy, but soon the strange commands made sense. And once he understood the logic behind the concepts, he didn't need all that much help—though he didn't let her know that. She was so genuinely pleased by his success that he made an effort to get to know her better.

Four months later he'd aced the course, and to celebrate, he'd asked her out on a date. And oh boy, had that been a mistake.

He rubbed his forehead. Twelve years later he still carried the scar to prove it.

Chapter Two

Sara opened her eyes just a slit, her head aching. She was on her back. Outside. Bright sunlight stabbed like an ice pick. She might have sunk back into a worry-free sleep, but a baby's cries pierced her pounding head like stinging nettles. "Abby?"

Just this once, Sara wanted to shut out the noise. Rest.

But Abby kept crying.

Unable to fall back into the darkness, memories and fear inundated her. The plane plunging downward. Holding Abby's hand. The cracking of treetops. Spinning. Rolling. Sliding. Snow…

Sara steeled herself against the brightness and peeked through narrowed eyelids. No wonder her head ached like someone had pulverized her brains—she was practically upside down. With her shoulders below her feet, she turned her head and craned her neck—to find herself positioned on the edge of a precipice. She squeezed her eyes shut in terror.

Another few inches and she'd plunge hundreds of feet over the cliff to certain death. Abby's wails told her she couldn't just lie there in the snow. She had to do something.

Forcing air into her lungs, Sara tested her limbs for pain. Assorted bruises. A humongous headache. Which would all end—if she slid over the cliff.

She could still hear Abby's cries, although her baby wasn't in sight. But she was alive. They were both alive.

The realization of how lucky they'd been to live at all gave Sara the courage to look around. Her jacket had ripped, then snagged, on a jagged outcropping of rock. Her jeans were damp and cold, her boots filled with snow, and her hand was wedged in a fork of jutting tree roots, preventing her from sliding farther down the almost vertical slope.

Now what?

She had to free herself. Had to get to Abby. But how?

Sara knew nothing about surviving in the wild, but she'd lived with Kirk long enough to realize that the most important thing to do was keep her wits about her. Where was he when she needed him? Same place he'd always been when she needed him. With his other family—the United States Marine Corps.

Yet, it was odd. As if Kirk were beside her, she could hear him speaking in that calm voice of his that never sounded panicked, no matter how critical the circumstances. *"Assess the situation."*

"I'm lying on the edge of a cliff in the middle of the friggin' Rocky Mountains." Snow seeped into her collar and down her back. Her fingers clasping the icy root were losing strength, starting to slip.

Abby screamed. "Mama. Mama."

And Sara found the strength to re-grip the root and hook her leg around it for extra support. Now she could free her hand.

"Don't rest on your laurels," she heard Kirk encouraging her. *"Pull yourself up for a look."*

"I can't!"

"You going to let that baby die, Sara?"

Abby was damn well not going to die. She was only eight months old. She wasn't even supposed to be here.

Clenching her jaw, using every bruised muscle in her body, Sara swung into a sitting position. Her efforts not only made her head feel a bit better, but she could fully open her eyes and search her surroundings without the sun streaming directly into her eyes.

Where was Abby?

Sara saw no metal parts. No smoke. Nothing but trees and sky and snow.

Grabbing one of the jagged rocks, Sara pulled herself back up the slope. Pain in her fingertips reached the excruciating level, and she used it—dug deep inside herself for strength, and climbed. Sara might not be accustomed to overcoming physical pain, but she knew all too well about the emotional kind. After her parents' deaths, she had grown sensitive to the fact that she was different from other children. She didn't have a mother or a father. She didn't wear nice clothes. She didn't take piano or ballet lessons. And when she got to high school, she didn't have friends.

She used the pain of loneliness to motivate herself to work hard in school. Fascinated by computers, she spent hours at the local college, making use of the school's Internet system. By her sophomore year, she could write basic programs. Some kids read science fiction books, other did drugs; Sara got lost in cyberspace.

At the start of her freshman year, Bobby Martinson asked her to meet him at the local burger hangout. He breezed into the fast-food place with a bunch of the popular kids and a pretty girl under his arm. And that was when Sara knew that Bobby Martinson had set her up to humiliate her.

She'd tried to sneak out the side door, but he hadn't allowed her to pretend she hadn't fallen for his trick. He and his group surrounded her. And then Bobby winked at his girlfriend.

''Waiting for someone special, Brain?''

''Obviously, he wasn't special enough,'' she had taunted right back. She had held her head high and squared her shoulders, but inside she'd raged. How dare he tell all his friends that he'd asked her out and then show up with another girl?

And why hadn't she suspected a trick? She should have known better. Boys didn't like her because she was smarter than they were. Girls thought she was a freak.

She really didn't care what the other kids thought. She didn't respect their opinions enough to care. But she figured she ought to have friends—someone whose opinions she did care about.

Bobby had leered at her, his expression mean. ''Maybe you could get a guy if you wore decent clothes.''

''Maybe you could get laid if you had a brain bigger than your dick.''

At her comment, the guys snickered, the girls

chuckled, and Bobby had looked confused but couldn't quite figure out if he'd been insulted or not. She took the opportunity to flee, but she couldn't escape her feelings of humiliation. And she had vowed she'd never let herself be that vulnerable again. She'd worked harder at her after-school jobs and studied longer to earn the scholarship she needed to attend college.

And just as the pain had fueled her ambitions in high school, she now used the raw pain in her hands and fingers to push herself another foot up the mountain.

Fighting and clawing for every bit of headway left her exhausted, but kept her warm, except for her fingers. Sara's muscles hurt in a dozen places, but ever so slowly, she fought the elements. Her lungs burning from lack of air, pulse racing as if she'd just run a mile, she was forced to stop and rest, and suddenly she realized something was very wrong. The sunlight seemed to mock her. The trees swayed.

Abby was no longer crying.

"IT'S IMPORTANT YOU REMEMBER that you aren't alone," Logan told Kirk during a break between phone calls. Headsets with microphones made conversation understandable despite the rotor noise from the chopper. "We'll supply backup, a base camp and everything from Pepper's favorite dog food to the latest intel, including entry into CIA, FBI and military databases."

"Who hired you?" Kirk asked.

"Black Hawk." Logan grinned. "It's the code

name for a secret government fund. Checks are cut out of Switzerland and totally deniable by Congress.''

Kirk still didn't understand why anyone was going to such expense to rescue Sara. He was grateful, but he needed to know why. ''Mind telling me why Black Hawk is paying your team to find Sara, a private citizen?''

''She's working on face-recognition software programs vital to the security of the United States.''

And Kirk knew somehow that Sara's programs would be far superior to the clumsy version available now. ''Let me guess. Sara was carrying the software with her when the plane went down, and our government is concerned that the software might fall into the wrong hands.''

Logan nodded. ''How familiar are you with Sara's work?''

''Last I heard, the face-recognition software was in the theoretical stage. She wanted her program to accurately map facial features in order to identify people in public places. Her theory is that facial bone structures are like fingerprints and can be used in many security applications.''

''She succeeded. While we are already using face-recognition software to prevent airline terrorism, the process is too slow and not accurate enough to be reliable. Sara's system is fast enough and precise enough to prove very useful to our country. Every division of law enforcement would like to implement her program.''

''So it would be extremely valuable,'' Kirk theorized, realizing that Sara was probably on the verge of becoming a very wealthy woman. "Is that where the protection part might become necessary?"

"Important people want to test her program—like every government in the free world. And terrorists. Plus her competition—tech companies that are at least three years behind her."

Who would have thought Sara and her computer could cause so much trouble? Or that her work would put her in mortal danger.

"Did your wife—"

"Ex-wife."

"Did she consult with other people?"

"Our divorce became final six months ago. I haven't spoken to her in almost a year and a half. I don't know what she's been doing recently or who she's been talking to." Kirk sighed. "But Sara's not a people person. She often worked alone for weeks at a time without talking to another soul."

"She sounds like an unusual woman."

Unusual? More like eccentric. And he'd once loved every eccentric inch of her. He thrust the memory aside. "I can tell you that she was always careful. When she worked on the Internet, she set up firewalls to protect her work and she never connected her primary computer to outside sources."

Logan increased airspeed, then gave Kirk a sideways glance. "You know where she stored her backups?"

Even if Kirk had known, he would not have admitted it. Fearing the government might consider recovering her work more important than rescuing the woman, Kirk wouldn't risk a mission recall.

Logan stared at him hard and, as if reading Kirk's

mind, tried to reassure him. "The funds for the search and rescue of Sara are already in the bank. I insist that payment be made up front on every mission. Even if we recover Sara's work, we won't leave her on that mountain. We don't leave good people behind. Not ever."

Logan sounded sincere. And Kirk wanted to believe him. But he wouldn't risk Sara's life on a stranger's word. Besides, Sara had always been careful. Kirk was sure she'd hidden her backup work someplace safe.

When it came to computers and her work, Sara always thought ahead. Always had a contingency plan.

Relating to other people was her problem. By the age of sixteen, Sara had learned how to defend herself against ridicule. Kids could be mean, but Sara's tongue was as sharp as her brilliant mind. After feeling the sting of one of her lashing comments, kids learned not to pick on her. She defended herself well.

With a grin of remembrance, Kirk rubbed the only visible scar she'd ever given him. After acing his computer course, he'd asked her to tutor him weekly for his other courses.

Sara knew how to pick out core ideas and had a knack for guessing what information the teachers would ask on their tests. By spring, her braces had finally come off and she'd been less self-conscious about smiling. And she'd finally saved enough money for a good haircut and more stylish clothes.

Sara's grandmother lived on social security, and taking in her grandchild had been a financial hardship. To make ends meet, they both worked odd jobs. Before school, Sara delivered newspapers. After school, she tutored students, then worked as a cashier at a local television repair shop. Sometimes, she took odd baby-sitting jobs.

She didn't have a boyfriend. Hell, she didn't even have a girlfriend—which should have told seventeen-year-old Logan to go slowly. At the time, he'd seen nothing dangerous about asking a girl on a date.

"If you have to work Friday, how about we hook up Saturday night?" he'd asked her at the end of his tutoring session in the school library.

She frowned at him. "You having trouble with biology?"

"I thought we could explore a little human biology. Together."

She sighed, ignoring his blatant innuendo. "Are you reading ahead? Mr. Scanlon won't get to those chapters until—"

"I'm trying to ask you out."

"Very funny." Sara gathered up papers and books and shoved them into her backpack.

"I'm serious."

"Yeah, right." She refused to look at him. "I thought that…"

"You thought that what?" Sara was never at a loss for words and that should have warned him.

"That you of all people would have enough respect for me not to play with my feelings."

What he wanted to do was play with her body. He already knew she had the most beautiful mind in the entire high school. He'd like to get to know more about what she hid beneath those baggy overalls. The girl had curves—in spades. But he couldn't exactly admit to her that for the past few months he'd fallen asleep hoping to dream about kissing her. She'd laugh in his face. A guy had to keep his pride.

That's when he decided that showing her his interest would be better than trying to tell her about it. She was standing close enough for him to take in the scent of her clean blond hair, which he longed to brush off her face. When he reached out and removed her glasses, her cute lips puckered in surprise.

Squinting at him, she grabbed for the glasses. "Give them back."

He jerked them out of her reach. "I want—"

"People are looking at us," she hissed.

"Let them."

And then the quarterback of the football team, the middle-distance track star and the state record holder of the five-hundred freestyle leaned forward and kissed The Brain. He never considered that she might reject him. Girls giggled when he walked by. His phone rang constantly with offers, but he wanted Sara. He figured she'd want him back—just like every other girl did.

He figured wrong.

His lips found hers. He draped an arm around her waist to draw her closer.

She stomped on his instep. Hard.

Pain shot through his foot and he muttered a curse. Leaning down, he clenched his aching foot, hopping on the good one. At the same time, she hefted her backpack onto her shoulder and swung around to make her exit. The backpack caught him over the eye, opening up a one-inch cut, and flattening him.

From his back, he raised his palm to the wound

above his eye. Blood rained down his cheek, making the injury appear much worse than it was. A freshman girl stepped around the bookcase and almost tripped over him before she screamed.

A teacher came running. Kids stared, pointing their fingers in blame. At Sara.

"She started it."

"She hit him."

"The Brain's going to get suspended."

She hadn't been suspended, of course, and the people in authority had sorted out the mess, which had gone down officially as an accident. Kirk's face had eventually healed. But every time he looked in the mirror, he remembered Sara, and the stark look of terrible confusion in her eyes as she'd fled the library.

Even back then, as an immature kid, he had realized that she'd misconstrued his intentions. She'd believed he was just like Bobby Martinson and that he'd kissed her to humiliate her. With a maturity beyond his years that came from genuine caring, he'd understood that The Brain couldn't imagine that he was for real, that his kiss was for real. With the blood dripping down his check, he'd suspected that of the pain suffered by the two of them, hers was worse.

And somehow he had to make her believe in him.

It had taken some time and a lot of effort, but eventually, he *had* made Sara believe in him—at least, for a while. Then he'd lost her to the divorce. As Kirk flew toward Sara in the chopper he tried not to think about whether he'd lost her for all eternity.

SARA STOOD on a plateau. Giant boulders towered on her left. A forest of pine trees grew in front of her and the surrounding peaks of other mountains loomed in every direction.

There was no sign of Abby. No sign of the plane. Yet her daughter had to be close. She'd heard her. But she'd also heard Kirk, and *he* definitely wasn't there. Had she been hallucinating Abby's cries, hearing what she wanted to hear?

Sara blew warm air on her hands. Upright, the wind plucked at her clothes, raced down her back, seeking openings in her clothing. She had to keep moving. Had to stay warm. Grateful for the thick jacket that she'd wrapped around her during the chilly plane ride, and for her warm snow boots, she was also thankful that she'd bundled Abby warmly. Sara shoved her cold hands into her jacket pockets, wishing she had gloves, and her hand struck smooth plastic.

Her cell phone!

With growing hope, she flipped open the lid. The fully charged battery lit up the LCD screen, making it easy for her to read the message. "No service."

Damn! The higher mountains surrounding her must be blocking the signal. Sara turned off the power to conserve the batteries, slipped the cell phone into her pocket and trudged through knee-deep snow. A whiff of fuel sent her hurrying toward thick underbrush, where she spied the car seat.

And Abby! Her baby appeared to be sleeping peacefully.

Sara lunged forward through the snow to her side. Tiny puffs of cold air came out of Abby's nose. Her pink cheeks were blotchy from crying, but she didn't have a scratch on her. It was as if fate had reached out a hand and set her daughter's car seat safely faceup, next to a large tree that kept her out of the chilling wind.

Now it was up to Sara to keep her alive.

Sara checked her first instinct, which was to scoop up her daughter and hold her against her chest. As much as she wanted to plant tiny kisses on Abby's neck, to tease her into a smile, to run her hands over her limbs to make sure nothing was broken, she couldn't give medical care to her daughter. She hadn't the knowledge or any supplies.

Damn the pilot who'd bailed with her stolen computer case. She hoped he'd broken his ankle on landing and was now sitting in a wet snowbank, shivering the way she was.

Sara forced herself to think, to set aside her own need to hold and breast-feed the baby. She had to focus on what she could do for them both.

Assess your situation. She recalled the words she'd thought Kirk had spoken. With only the bag full of diapers that attached to the car seat, an extra baby blanket and Sara's laptop, their most immediate concern was shelter. Building a fire.

Sara removed the blanket and several spare diapers. She packed the sides of the car seat with the diapers for extra insulation against the cold, then floated the blanket over the baby and tucked it around her with care. Sara needed warmth and protection from the elements more than her mother's kisses.

Darkness fell as early as four o'clock in the mountains. She had to construct a shelter and build a fire while it was still light.

Chapter Three

The nearest Sara had come to camping was watching the Travel Channel on cable television. With her limited gear and no food, walking out of the Rocky Mountains with the baby in her arms seemed impossible. The snow-covered, steep terrain made traversing even a few hundred yards treacherous, but she couldn't just sit next to Abby and wait for a rescue.

Her plane should have been landing in California about now and, while someone might notice their failure to arrive, it might be hours before the Federal Aviation Administration narrowed the crash area possibilities. Finding them in such a remote area would be difficult, as the plane was probably hidden by snow and trees. And she didn't believe she could count on a satellite pinpointing their location through her plane's black box—only commercial aircraft had that kind of gear.

Ignoring her rumbling stomach, she trudged toward the trees, dreaming of English muffins slathered with butter and jelly, following the faint scent of smoke, searching for the crashed airplane. Maybe she'd luck out, find a radio or an emergency locator beacon that she could activate.

Or extra blankets. Or food. Maybe she and Abby could use the plane for shelter.

And maybe she'd win the lottery.

A light snow had begun to fall, but her tracks were so deep she didn't fear forgetting her way back to her daughter. Clouds had closed in over the mountain, blocking the surrounding peaks from view and casting a dull gray light over the tiny flakes of falling snow. Gusts of wind caught the snow in eddies and whirls, and as if she didn't have enough trouble, she wondered if this light snow might be a precursor to a full-blown storm.

She trudged through the woods, reluctant to go too far from Abby, and saw no sign of the plane. About to give up and turn back, she took another few steps and almost tumbled over a precipice. Flinging her body sideways into a snowbank to avoid falling off the mountain, she scrambled away with just inches to spare.

Cold, bruised and growing more worried with each falling snowflake, she raised her hand to her forehead and blinked the snow off her eyelashes. There. Just below a rock outcropping and impossibly out of reach, she spied the plane's tail.

But where were the cockpit and the fuselage?

Careful not to crawl too close to the edge, Sara peered below. The tail section had sheered off and had fallen into a gulch. Already, a light frosting of snow covered the metal, camouflaging the silhouette's shape. It would not be spotted by anyone searching from the air.

As the wind picked up, Sara realized that no plane would be searching for them until this storm broke. And by then it might be too late.

Don't go there.

Primitive peoples had survived winters in the mountains. She and Abby should be able to last one night. If she couldn't get to the airplane, she would have to make do with the resources she had.

Think, Sara. What did the Inuit do?

They built igloos!

Well, she had plenty of snow, but no gloves. She retraced her steps toward Abby, realizing that with her back to the wind, she was warmer. Okay, build the shelter in a spot out of the wind.

The lowest branches of some trees almost touched the ground, forming a natural tent around the base of the trunk. If she could use those branches to help mold her igloo, she'd have a head start on the walls of her shelter and part of a roof already done.

Two hours later, exhausted and extremely hungry, Sara shoved Abby and her car seat into the makeshift edifice. It wasn't pretty. It wasn't warm, but it was the best she could do with the materials on hand. And it had been damn hard work. Sara fought to keep her eyes open, but her baby was hungry and just one gurgle from Abby set Sara's breasts leaking.

She rested her back again the tree trunk, sat on a stump she'd found, held Abby under her coat and bared her breast. Abby latched onto her nipple and sucked strongly. At least she could feed her baby until her milk ran out.

Eating snow chilled Sara. If only they had a fire— but she had no matches. No magnifying glass or lens to start a spark from focused sunlight—not that there was enough left with the clouds that were closing in.

Sara switched Abby to her other breast, and at the dropping temperature, she shivered. If Kirk were here, they'd no doubt have a cheery fire going. But he wasn't here, and she'd made up her mind she and Abby could get on with their lives without him. That's what she'd been telling herself ever since their divorce. And it was true—she could manage just fine in the civilized world without Kirk Hardaker. Which didn't mean that she didn't miss him, or turn to reach for him in the middle of the night before she remembered that he was no longer hers.

Even when they'd been married, he hadn't been hers. That had been the problem. Kirk's other family—the Marine Corps—took precedence. She'd loved him enough to put up with his long, unexplained absences. What she couldn't live with was the fear of knowing how he spent his days and nights—searching for bombs to keep overseas embassies, offices or training centers safe. All too often, he and his dogs found what they were looking for, and he had the scars on his body to prove it.

Often Kirk couldn't even tell her about his missions. But she'd kept track by his scars. A truck bomb in Panama had left a pucker from hot flying metal on his right thigh. Thanks to a mission to Haiti, he had forty stitches in his scalp that his hair covered, but that she knew were there. Desert Storm and Yugoslavia had given him a nasty chest wound and a cut on his ear.

Only God and the U.S. Marine Corps knew where he was now.

Since their divorce, a year and a half ago, she'd tried oh-so-hard not to think of Kirk, the marriage they'd once had and the memories they shared, which she still found so painful. She'd thrown herself into her work and taking care of Abby, and tried never to think of her failure to come to terms with Kirk's dangerous occupation.

She hoped Kirk was warmer than she was. She'd shoved a rotted stump into her makeshift igloo to sit on, but her butt felt numb with cold. After Abby finished eating, Sara changed her diaper, then kept the baby under her jacket for shared body warmth.

Body heat wasn't enough. Rocking back and forth to keep her blood circulating wasn't enough. But what more could Sara do when her supplies consisted of spare diapers, a car seat and her laptop? She'd better come up with an idea soon or they might not survive through the night.

KIRK AND LOGAN LANDED the chopper in Detroit and transferred to a private plane, a 727 outfitted with enough electronic equipment to give Kirk an idea of the variety and scope of the missions Logan's team took on.

Pepper sniffed the air, found a warm space between a leather sofa and a wall, curled up and snoozed.

Logan made the introductions. ''Jack Donovan, Kirk Hardaker.''

The pilot, tall and lanky, shook hands. ''Welcome aboard.'' He had a warm southern accent, a firm handshake and a keen eye, and he sized up Kirk and Pepper in one sharp glance.

''How's the weather?'' asked Kirk.

The pilot eased into his seat, his gaze sweeping over his instrument panel. "We're good to go."

"Is anyone else besides us flying into the storm?" Logan asked Jack.

Jack winked at Logan. "I'll get us there safe and sound, boss."

Kirk noticed that the pilot didn't answer their questions, but relieved that the man seemed determined to fly through bad weather if necessary, Kirk strapped on a seat belt and accepted a headset from Logan. While the headsets weren't as necessary in the relatively quiet plane as they were inside the chopper, the sheer size of this aircraft limited communication. With the headset, the men could speak to one another easily from within any part of the fuselage or connect to radio and phone networks through the cockpit.

Jack spoke to both men through the headsets. "We're starting to receive intel from Ryker."

"Ryker Stevens is ex-special forces with a master's degree in business," Logan explained. "His specialty in cracking the secrets of financial statements and balance sheets has solved many a case." Logan spoke into the mouthpiece. "Ryker, what have you got?"

The conversation suddenly became a four-way conference call as Ryker spoke. "Sara Hardaker was about to sell her software to the U.S. government for millions of dollars."

Kirk winced. Only Sara would carry something so valuable around without even a bodyguard to protect her. And she was one of the most unobservant people he knew. Once she lost herself in her intricate calculations and programs, she wouldn't notice day turning to night, or that she hadn't eaten or answered her phone. A stranger could openly tail her, and she'd never notice. He couldn't imagine her as a mother, wasn't sure he wanted to try.

"Backup copies?" Logan asked as the plane taxied down the runway and smoothly lifted into the cloudy Michigan skies. The Great Lakes area didn't offer many sunny days during winter, and today was no exception. Raining, at thirty-three degrees, the weather was the kind that made you want to curl up with a good book before a roaring fire, with a faithful dog at your side. But staying home wasn't an option. Not with Sara lost in the Rocky Mountains.

Ryker's voice, precise and clear, reported to his boss. "If Sara made backups of her work, she hid them well. Or the software may already have been stolen. Her house was trashed. A professional job. No prints. Nothing seemed to have been taken, not even a gold watch left in a jewelry box on the bedroom dresser."

Kirk had given her the watch for an engagement present. She'd been so happy with his gift, and now it sounded as if she didn't wear it anymore. Throw away the man, throw away his present. Only, she'd kept the watch—for sentimental reasons?

Kirk felt like an eavesdropper. Worse, he was annoyed these men had invaded Sara's bedroom, gone through her things. She was a private person who liked her own space.

He hadn't realized that in the almost year and a half since their divorce she'd moved from the Detroit apartment to a house. He thought of the baby and frowned. Apparently there were quite a few things he didn't know about Sara anymore. How old was the baby? She certainly hadn't wasted any time finding a new relationship. Who was the father?

"What else have you got for me?" Logan asked.

"Nothing yet on the pilot. He used a fake name and address, so we don't have much to go on. The company that hired him seems as baffled by his identity as we are. He had no close friends and cashed his company checks at the local bank. The account's been closed."

"Sounds like a dead end," Kirk muttered.

"Maybe not," Ryker countered, seemingly not the least surprised by a stranger's voice on the channel. "We got his prints off his stolen car and we're running them through AFIS."

"Good. Logan out." Logan cut the connection, unsnapped his seat belt and motioned for Kirk to follow him. Kirk signaled for Pepper to stay, then he headed aft toward the electronics section.

A map of the entire country, which looked much like the weatherman's map on the evening television news, dominated one computer screen. Logan traced an area over the Rocky Mountains with his index finger.

"Cold weather's moving in. Looks like snow—and lots of it."

Seeing the size of the weather system, Kirk felt a ball of ice freezing his gut at the hopelessness of Sara's situation. With a strong effort of will, he focused on the positive. The pilot was willing to fly into that massive storm. The man was either courageous or an idiot, but Kirk was grateful that these men were willing to put their lives on the line to save Sara. They would have to land in the snow and the dark, in the middle of whiteout conditions.

''I've brought snow booties for Pepper to keep her feet from freezing.'' Kirk didn't mention that search and rescue missions at night were fraught with danger. When neither man nor dogs could see well, it was too easy to make a mistake—especially in rough terrain. Going out in a snowstorm would be bad, but for Sara and her baby, Kirk would try. ''You have any idea where her plane went down?''

''Near here.'' Logan circled an area in the mountains with his finger. ''I'm hoping to pinpoint that information by the time we land in Colorado. Jack will fly us to base camp and another chopper's on standby in Denver. ETA is after sundown.''

''I'm heading out the moment we arrive.''

''Not 'til daylight.''

Kirk shook his head. ''Daylight will be too late. The mountain air's going to drop below freezing tonight. And if she's at any kind of altitude, the temperature could fall below zero.''

''Does Sara have any survival skills?'' Logan asked, his voice deep with concern.

Survival skills? Sara couldn't remember to check the gas gauge in her car. The Sara that Kirk had married had trouble surviving in a fully equipped kitchen. She knew when supper was done when the smoke detector went off. It wasn't that she was a rotten cook, she just couldn't seem to stay in the kitchen long enough to see the preparation through to the end. She'd fix the food, then while she waited for it to cook, she'd wander over to her computer and wouldn't look up until the apartment was filled with a burning smell. He imagined the baby had to cry to get fed.

At the thought of the baby, Kirk realized he'd put off asking Logan the vital question. He'd been slowly working up the courage ever since Logan mentioned Abby by name. But Kirk suddenly couldn't wait another moment to know the truth.

"How old is the baby?"

Logan didn't need to check the file. He raised an eyebrow, but his voice remained level. "Eight months."

Eight months old, plus nine months in the womb. Seventeen months ago had been spring. And he'd been home on leave with Sara.

Abby was his child.

Kirk had a daughter and Sara had never told him. Happiness and pride, sorrow and anger stirred inside him in the oddest combination. Why hadn't Sara told him? He had a right to know about the child—even if the mother had divorced him.

As Kirk stared at the massive snowstorm blowing down from the northern states and Canada, he realized that he might never learn the truth. He didn't know if Sara and Abby had survived the crash, but if they had, unless they found shelter and a way to start a fire, they wouldn't survive the night.

He refused to believe she was dead. However, he had no rational basis for that thought. None.

Sara might be the most brilliant woman he'd ever met, but she was totally out of her element. Absent-minded when involved in her work—and she was always working—Sara had to be reminded to put on her boots before going out in the snow. With a computer, the woman was sheer genius, but he shuddered at the idea of her alone on a mountain even during a warm summer rain.

And Sara wasn't alone. She had a baby to take care of. And a huge snowstorm coming in.

He dialed her cell phone and prayed she would answer. The computer message that the customer was unavailable at this time made him feel like throwing his phone into the plane's wall in frustration. Instead, he pocketed the cell phone and told himself to have faith. In Sara. In fate. In some greater power that wouldn't allow him to learn he had a daughter, only to snatch her away.

SARA HUGGED ABBY, who had fallen back to sleep after her meal. With the pine branches and snow walls of her igloo cutting the wind, she'd protected them as best she could from the elements.

The last time she'd been out in snow like this was in college. She and Elaine had been studying in the stacks of the University of Michigan's huge library. They'd been inside for hours, and when they exited late that Saturday night, the wind forced the women to keep their heads down as they trudged through the darkness.

"There's a party in West Quad," Elaine shouted above the storm. "Let's stop in."

Parties weren't Sara's idea of fun. Too much loud music, not enough good conversation. However, her face felt frozen and she'd welcome the warmth. Besides, she had decided she needed to get out more.

College had opened up a whole new and exciting world for Sara. Although most of the computer sci-

ence majors were men, she'd found a few other
women with interests similar to her own. She'd dis-
covered not only that she wasn't a freak, but that she
had a mind other students admired. Sara had made a
few friends.

Although she was far from classifying herself as a
party animal, she dated occasionally. She had a social
life, and she was mostly content. Busy maintaining
her four-point average to keep her academic scholarship, she also worked part-time tutoring other students.

So when Elaine grabbed her arm and dragged her
into the dorm, Sara didn't protest. The indoor heat
relaxed her as they followed the beat of music to the
party. Sara removed her hat, shoved it into her pocket
and had started to unbutton her jacket, when a familiar guy rounded the corner of the room.

Kirk Hardaker.

She hadn't seen him since high school. His lanky
body had filled out with very masculine muscles.
She'd heard he had been admitted to U of M on a
full swimming scholarship, but on the huge campus
their paths had never crossed.

Until now.

While he might still be a jock and she might still
be a brain, she had learned more social skills. With
only a slight skip of her heart, she shot Kirk a friendly
grin. "Hi."

Okay, maybe "hi" wasn't brilliant dialogue and
just a bit awkward. She could get over awkward—but
only if he remembered her. If he didn't recognize her,
she would just keep walking into the crowded room
and right out the back door.

"Sara?" Kirk strode over without hesitation. "Damn, you look good."

"Thanks. You don't look so bad yourself."

"Let me get you a beer." He placed a casual arm over her shoulder and steered her toward a keg. Elaine disappeared into the room with a casual wave of her hand, leaving Sara to fend for herself. Not that she minded.

Kirk had been her first friend in high school, and she'd always regretted that when he'd tried to kiss her, she'd knocked him flat on his back. And now, after all this time, fate had given her an opportunity to make amends.

She sipped the beer and stared up into his steady eyes, which she still found inviting. Taking a deep breath, she reminded herself that nothing ventured, nothing gained. "You know, I've always wanted to apologize for hitting you. I thought you were setting me up."

"I figured that out—too late."

He rubbed the scar over his brow, and she recalled his bloody face with a wince that made him chuckle.

"You left your mark on me," he added.

"Sorry."

His eyes glimmered with amusement. "You know what I'm sorry about?"

"What?"

"That I never found out what it would have been like to kiss you."

Her stomach flip-flopped, and she looked around, expecting a cheerleader or homecoming queen to appear and claim him.

As if reading her mind, he grinned. "I came alone."

She'd forgotten how perceptive he was. "You're not seeing anyone?"

He shook his head. "Are you?"

"Nope."

He took her plastic cup of mostly untouched beer from her hand and set it down. "Want to dance?"

She hadn't even felt the cold when they left the party together. Kirk had always had that effect on her. He kept her warm and feeling protected and cherished.

She wished he were on the mountain with her now.

But he wasn't. Kirk was off on a mission, probably halfway around the world, and couldn't possibly know that Sara and his daughter would likely freeze to death before morning. And yet, while she would have appreciated his survival skills, she didn't really want to see him. Seeing him would bring back too much pain—especially his rejection of Abby.

Not for the first time she wondered why he'd never answered her letters telling him about her pregnancy. She'd written twice, and when he hadn't responded, she'd been forced to conclude that he didn't care. Maybe he'd thought she didn't deserve a response because she'd divorced him. Maybe he didn't care, and that hurt most of all. He'd always put the military before her, and now he'd done the same to Abby, excising them both from his life as if they didn't exist. When Kirk had finally called after Abby's birth, she'd been too angry and hurt to talk to him, but now she regretted her decision. If she and Abby died on the mountain, she wanted Kirk to know about his daughter's birth, her first smile, her first word.

If she couldn't talk to Kirk, she could at least write him one last letter. She could tell him about the wonderful baby they had made together....

Sara refused to cry. She didn't have the luxury of wasting the liquid of tears, not when Abby might need her breast milk in another few hours.

Swallowing the lump of sorrow in her throat, Sara slipped the specialized laptop out of the plastic pocket of the diaper bag and flipped on the machine. Automatically, she checked the power. Even with the cold, she had enough juice left in the battery to last for hours.

And then, as with every brilliant idea that seemed to come out of her subconscious, she suddenly thought of a way to stay alive. The battery had power!

Knowing she needed to work quickly, Sara placed Abby back into her car seat and covered her with the blanket. ''Mommy's going to make us a fire, darling.''

Sara shut down the laptop, flipped over her casing and unscrewed the back with a twig. Knowing that she was destroying one-of-a-kind technology, she ripped out the wires between the motherboard and the hard drive, then removed the battery. She could always rebuild the hardware—if she lived long enough.

She attached the leads to the battery with her fingers and was about to cross the wires to test the spark, but stopped. She had no idea how many times the battery would spark. She might only get one chance, and she couldn't waste it.

She needed kindling, but there was none to be had

in her makeshift igloo. Her gaze fell on Abby's diapers. She had none to spare. However, she could use Abby's soiled one, the one she'd buried only a few minutes ago. The padding at the top of the used diaper was dry, and she tore it from the plastic. Next she gathered pine needles and small twigs from the tree.

But she needed wood. While the stump would burn if she could make the fire hot enough, Sara needed thin branches to start out with and she didn't dare not have them ready to go when she created her tiny flame. Nothing would be worse than kindling the spark, starting a tiny fire and then running out of fuel.

She didn't want to leave Abby. Didn't want to go out into the storm. But she had no choice.

Sara crawled under the branches and through the small opening she'd left in the walls made of snow. Bitter wind whipped her face and lashed at her jacket.

As cold as it was inside her fort, outside was frigid. And dark. If there was a moon, she couldn't see it behind the storm clouds. Snow stung her face, and she dipped her head down to avoid the full blast in her eyes.

Don't get lost. Mark your trail. Abby is counting on you to come back.

Sara fought her way to the dead tree she'd found earlier. With her boot, she cracked small branches from the trunk and set them in a pile. She made four trips with her arms full of branches and then made three more, rolling and dragging the thicker pieces that were too heavy to carry.

This might be her only chance to gather wood. The storm might last another forty-eight hours. When she couldn't take another step, she stopped gathering wood.

Exhausted and freezing, she finally crawled back into the snow fort. In the darkness, she couldn't see Abby's coloring, but the baby's breathing sounded steady. Sara dragged in her collected branches, leaving the bigger stuff outside but within reach.

The moment to test her fire-making ability had arrived. But it was now pitch-dark. She dried her hands on the inside of her shirt, and held the wires to the battery with the free ends over the diaper stuffing by feel rather than using her sight. Then she crossed the wires.

"Spark, damn it. Give me a spark."

Chapter Four

With a heavy heart, Kirk watched the weather system blanket Colorado. In blizzard-like conditions, their ex-military chopper pilot, Jack Donovan, agreed, with a cocky nod, to fly them to base camp—but Logan okayed the mission only because lives were at stake. Kirk's respect for Logan Kincaid rose several notches when he insisted on riding along and endangering his own life. Clearly, Logan didn't just sit behind his desk. He took a hands-on approach to his business.

"This *is* my operation," Logan told him with one of those level looks that probably made subordinates immediately cease all arguments.

"Look, I appreciate the help," Kirk shouted into the wind, as the three men and Pepper ran toward the chopper at the Denver airport, "but you needn't risk your life, too."

"I'm going."

Since Logan had made all the arrangements, Kirk couldn't exactly kick the man off the mission. They took their seats, and Jack got immediate clearance from the tower to take off. "Strap in. Ride's going to be bumpy.'' He sounded cheerful, as if he looked forward to the challenge.

Logan and Kirk strapped in, then Logan dialed and spoke into his cell phone. ''Have we got her location yet?''

Kirk held his breath, trying to read Logan's expression. The man didn't give away much. Probably out of habit. But the answer to his question was critical. The Rocky Mountains covered a vast area. Without knowing exactly where to look, he might take weeks to find Sara and their baby. Even if the FAA narrowed down the crash area to one square mile, if Sara and the child were buried by snow, finding them could take days. And they had only hours.

Logan snapped his phone shut. ''We have an eyewitness who pegged the crash site.''

Some good news for a change. ''Did he see the plane go down? Was there an explosion?''

''Apparently, the plane struck an outcropping of rock. Debris shot two clouds of dust into the air.''

''Two?''

''Experts have told me this indicates that the plane probably broke into two pieces on impact. Hence, two dust clouds. Satellites would have picked up any explosion. None was reported.''

''How close can you get me to the site?'' Kirk asked.

''About a third of the way up the mountain. The plane crashed below the timberline, close to the peak. The air's too thin to fly the chopper and land above the site. And below is a steep grade covered by trees. The only areas devoid of trees aren't suitable landing sites—either too steep or strewn with boulders.''

"What about dropping Pepper and me down from a rope? The dog has a harness."

"We couldn't even attempt it tonight. Too much wind." Logan must have sensed that Kirk was about to argue and placed a calming hand on his shoulder. "Look, we want her found as soon as possible, too. But you won't do her a lick of good if you go in and bash your brain into a tree."

As if to emphasize the strength of the blizzard outside, the chopper hit an air pocket and then a gust of wind lifted them. Jack muttered, fighting to keep the craft level. Kirk scratched Pepper behind the ears, proud that she took the roller-coaster ride like a pro.

Kirk considered climbing the mountain from base camp, but the storm was so intense that he couldn't see out two feet past the chopper's window. He marveled that Jack could wrestle the chopper into flying at all. Sara had picked one helluva night to spend on a mountain. He prayed she wasn't injured—knew she would use that super-smart brain of hers to save herself and the baby if she could. She had a way of coming up with brilliant solutions to problems that other people didn't so much as understand, never mind solve. Back in college she not only had excelled as a student, but had overcome many of her high school insecurities.

They'd been dating for two years when he decided to enter the military, and she'd supported him fully. She'd had only one condition.

"Marry me, Kirk."

He snapped his fingers. "Now, why didn't I think of that?"

She scowled at him but her tone teased. "Because

you believe I'm not strong enough to keep loving you while you're gone?''

That wasn't his concern and she knew it. He didn't think it was fair for a woman to tie herself to a man who wasn't home very often.

''As long as I can hook into the Internet, I can work anywhere.'' She trailed her hand down one arm. ''Say yes.'' And then she pulled the trump card. ''I need you, Kirk. I need a family....''

Her grandmother had died during her junior year. The woman who had lived so frugally had left her granddaughter a car and a house with no mortgage. But she'd also left Sara with an emptiness in her heart.

How could Kirk say no? He loved Sara. And in this day and age, he told himself, a man didn't have to choose between a military career and a wife.

He'd bought her a pearl engagement ring, the kind she thought pretty. Diamonds are cold, she told him. Pearls glow with warmth.

Between graduation and their marriage plans, they'd been busy and happy. That summer when he'd left her for boot camp, she'd been fine. And she'd gone with him when he'd been stationed in Panama.

She couldn't go with him to Yugoslavia or the Middle East, and that's when she started pressing him about starting a family. He kept putting her off. Her work was at a critical stage. She worked sixty to seventy hours a week. She didn't have time to take care of a baby, and he wasn't home.

But the debate over whether to start a family hadn't been the reason their marriage fell apart. She had been working so hard to drive her worries out of her mind. Worries about him.

Working with his dog to sniff out bombs was dangerous. He'd had several injuries, a few close calls. And she'd worried over his safety to the point where she made herself sick. She lost weight, didn't sleep, claimed she had nightmares about losing him—and had begged him to quit. Come home. Live with her and make a baby.

He'd refused. And she had divorced him. For a while he'd felt as though she'd sliced off his right arm. Eventually, the wound grew numb—but it had never healed.

Then, two days after he'd sent Abby the signed divorce papers, his partner and friend Gabby had died. A bomb had exploded in the building he was searching. With the passage of time and Kirk's success in tracking down the terrorists that had killed his best friend, his grief over Gabby's death had eased. And working with a new partner and on a new mission, he'd expected life to return to normal.

But his divorce had haunted him. Without Sara at home waiting for him, the joy had gone out of his life. He no longer took pleasure in the adventure of his job, no longer took satisfaction in his successes. Without Sara, his life seemed meaningless. And that's when he knew that she had been right. It was time to quit. He'd had to just finish his hitch, which had taken almost another year.

He had made his decision too late, it turned out. He'd already lost Sara. He'd tried to phone, but she hadn't taken his calls. He'd left messages that she never answered. And he finally got *her* message. She didn't want to talk to him, to see him.

And now he knew she'd gone and had the baby without him. He couldn't believe she'd never told him. There wasn't a duplicitous bone in Sara's body. He'd sooner believe that she'd gotten so wrapped up in her work that she'd simply forgotten to tell him. But not even Sara was that absentminded.

Nevertheless, the question ate away at him like acid. Why hadn't she told him that he had a daughter?

"IF ONLY YOUR DAD could see us now." Sara's voice came to Kirk so clearly and loudly that it woke him from his dream.

Kirk sat up with a start and took his bearings. The skilled chopper pilot had safely landed them at base camp in the middle of a blizzard. Even in the protected valley, the fierce winds had made last night's landing hazardous, but Jack had whistled through his teeth and set them down with only a minor *thud*. They'd had to fight their way to the tents that stood protected in the lee of a cliff.

Kirk had eaten a self-heating meal that the army used for rations, he'd fed Pepper, and then he'd settled into his down sleeping bag for the night. Despite the long day, despite his need to sleep so he could get an early start if the storm broke, he had tossed and turned.

And dreamed of Sara cuddling their baby in front of a warm fire. A sign from heaven? Or wishful thinking?

Either way, he tried to hold on to the image. Although she'd divorced him, he liked thinking that

Sara was happy and warm and safe. He'd never really understood how she'd felt during their marriage. While he may have laid his life on the line every day, she had to worry that he'd never return. Until now, he hadn't comprehended what it felt like to have his guts tied into rigid knots with worry. Not knowing if she was alive or wounded or suffering felt like an acute stab wound to the gut, a pounding hammer on the brain. And she'd lived with that kind of intense pressure every day and night, while he'd searched for bombs, often in hostile countries.

Every time they said goodbye, either in person, by phone, or by e-mail, she'd never known if she would hear from him again. That she'd lived with that kind of pressure for so many years only revealed her inner strength. He could no longer blame Sara for ending their marriage.

The uncertainty of the past twenty hours had him ready to charge into the blizzard. Sara had gotten lost in her work to escape worrying about him. And that she'd loved her computer did little to ease his mind— especially when that very same work might be the reason she was up on that mountain.

Kirk cracked his knuckles and barely refrained from howling at the storm. Pepper, sensitive as always to his moods, thrust her muzzle into his palm. Absently, he scratched behind her ears. Her soft *woof* warned him that someone approached.

"Over here," Kirk shouted, knowing the wind would muffle his words but hoping to lead whoever was out there to the shelter of his tent with as few missteps as possible.

A minute later, Logan entered the tent, handed him

a mug of coffee, then zipped the tent behind him. "Figured you might be up."

"Appreciate the coffee." Kirk sipped, settled onto his cot and gestured toward the only chair.

Pepper curled on her blanket at the foot of his cot. Calm and quiet, she was excellent about accepting people and had been trained to obey commands from other handlers. But there was a special bond between them that came from working together over a period of time. She would stay down on the cot until he signaled her by hand or voice that it was okay to move. Right now, she needed to rest. Their journey probably wouldn't be long, but he suspected it would prove arduous.

"Any break in the weather?" Kirk asked Logan.

"Maybe in the next hour."

"I'm good to go." Kirk took out a sweater of Sara's that Logan had given him. She'd kept it wrapped in one of those clear plastic bags that gets thrown into the back of a closet and forgotten. He let Pepper take a few good sniffs. "Pepper's the best search dog I've ever worked with. Since we already have a very good idea where the plane went down, Pepper should have little trouble picking up the scent. And…"

"And you want to be the one who finds her?" Logan asked with a perceptiveness that made Kirk very glad this man wasn't an enemy.

"I'd like to be the one to find her, yes. Handlers are a tough breed. We have to keep up, running and swimming beside our dogs for hours, but climbing snow-covered mountains is beyond the abilities of all but the most experienced of us."

"Why?"

"I may have to climb bare rock with just my hands and feet. Then I've got to have the strength to haul my dog up, too. We usually don't carry much gear, but in these conditions, I'll need to carry extra supplies. A blanket for Pepper so she has a warm place to rest. Food for her. A radio. Emergency first aid equipment."

"And a gun."

Kirk snapped his head up. He wished in the dim light of the oil lamp that he could see Logan's face better. "You think that if Sara survived, whoever made her plane go down might try again?"

"It's only a possibility. But I like to go in prepared for every contingency."

"I don't want to pack more than the absolute essentials."

"Agreed. Once you find the crash site, the chopper may be able to air-drop whatever you need."

If the weather cooperated.

Neither man stated the obvious. That Sara and the baby might have died in the crash. That Kirk might be risking his life in a futile mission. However, if there was the slimmest chance that she was still alive, he had to go. And if she hadn't made it, he wanted her death to count for something meaningful. If Sara's face-recognition software could make their country safe by keeping out terrorists, Kirk, with Logan's help, would see that the right people got it.

Logan removed a satchel from his shoulder and tossed it onto the cot. "Things you might need."

The handgun was on top. Kirk removed the gun

from an underarm holster, checked the load and the safety. "Extra ammo?"

"Clipped to the back strap of the holster."

Kirk reached into the bag and pulled out several soft and plastic somethings. "Diapers."

"And powdered formula. While Sara is breast-feeding—"

"And you know that because?"

"One of my men accessed her medical records from her doctor's computer."

Damn him. Logan had no right to invade Sara's privacy. And yet, Kirk couldn't fault the man. If Kirk climbed that mountain and arrived to find a hungry baby that Sara couldn't feed, he'd be grateful for the dried formula. He merely needed to melt snow, pour the packet into the bottle and shake.

He almost didn't want to empty the rest of the items, but he forced himself. A sling to carry a baby. Gloves and heavy socks for Sara. A wad of cash?

"The only thing that money is good for on that mountain is burning it for warmth."

"None of my men go on a mission without cash."

Kirk didn't point out that he wasn't one of Logan's men. No doubt cash was a great contingency item—in most cases. But in the middle of the Rocky Mountains? "Look, it's not that I don't appreciate the gesture, but I'm already packing too much weight. And if I find them alive, I may have to carry them out."

"You aren't going without the gun or the cash."

"Fine." He'd sensed from the start that he'd have to do this Logan's way or no way. He might have to take Logan's supplies, but Kirk refrained from saying that he didn't have to come back with either the gun or the cash.

"There's one other thing. I want you to maintain radio silence until you call the chopper in for a rescue or unless there's an emergency."

"You really think someone is out there trying to stop us from getting to Sara?"

Logan's voice was grim. "I think they may try and beat you in recovering her work."

"How do you know they didn't get the information they wanted from her home?"

"They trashed her home *after* the plane went down—which may indicate that they haven't found the program. Obviously they still are searching. However, it's also possible they simply wanted to ensure that they had accounted for every copy of her program."

"But you think whoever crashed her plane made a mistake? That they tried to kill Sara before they stole her work?"

"It's possible. And my team examined her computer's hard drive. She wiped it clean—but if they'd found anything on it, they would have stolen it. I'm thinking they probably expected to steal the work off her hard drive at home."

"You're guessing, aren't you?"

Logan nodded. "Guessing right is what I do best."

As soon as the blizzard had slowed Kirk and Pepper headed out. The pressure of a real mission was different from a training run, and Pepper lost her relaxed demeanor and got down to it, bounding with eager leaps through the snow and lifting Kirk's spirits.

The German shepherd obviously enjoyed both her work and her strong rapport with him. And she was special. She didn't really require a scent article, but since Logan had produced Sara's sweater, Kirk had let her take in a good whiff. Pepper didn't need tracks, or a starting point for her keen senses to locate Sara.

Even the best handlers weren't sure how the dogs tracked scent. Probably the scent carried in downward wind spirals in a widening cone shape. Pepper would zigzag back and forth until she picked up the scent, then hone in on it.

But first they needed to climb the mountain and get closer to the crash site. Signaling Pepper to stay close, he and the dog moved as a team and at a steady pace. After an hour Kirk broke into a light sweat, but his specialized clothing wicked away moisture from his skin. Pepper wore booties to protect her feet from freezing or being cut as they climbed rough terrain and patches of ice.

Sometimes the snow reached Kirk's hips, other times he walked across slippery rocks, and once he took advantage of trail broken by large animals, probably deer. At first he barely noticed the additional weight of his pack, but after three hours, the straps cut into his shoulders. Kirk considered but resisted throwing away the gun and the cash that Logan had insisted he take with him. He stopped to rest and drink, giving Pepper water and a treat.

Kirk used his GPS, which told him his location within a few feet and kept him on a direct path upward. "Another hour, girl."

Pepper wagged her tail, raised her head and sniffed. She let out a low whine that indicated her eagerness to keep going, to do the work she spent so much time training for.

"Rest a little first," Kirk told her. "We'll make better time if we—"

A shot fired, echoing across the mountain. A patch of snow from above them broke off the mountainside and plunged toward where Pepper and Kirk stood. The miniature avalanche missed them by less than fifty yards.

Pepper growled and Kirk dived for cover, knowing she'd automatically stay with him. He had no idea if someone had fired at him and missed, or if a hunter's stray shot had gone awry. Either way, he didn't want to present himself or Pepper as a target.

Another possibility crossed his mind. Sara might have found a gun on the plane and tried to signal for help, firing close but not too close.

However, it was much more likely that Logan had been right. That someone else wanted to stop Kirk from getting to Sara first.

He had no idea from where the shot had been fired and hesitated to risk coming out from behind the tree. He listened hard and heard nothing. No footsteps. No cracking branches. No voices. Just the wind and Pepper's panting.

And Sara's voice in his head, urging him to hurry.

Kirk removed his hat, placed it over a branch and stuck it out from behind the tree, prepared to pull back at the first sign of danger. But nothing happened.

However, he had not imagined that shot. He considered breaking radio silence, but decided against doing so. Logan had warned him to use the radio only in an emergency. While a shot fired at him might qualify, calling in for information or help might allow whoever was out there to triangulate on his position.

Kirk couldn't allow anyone to reach Sara before he did and, with renewed determination, he headed upward. Choosing his path to take advantage of natural cover slowed him more than he would have liked, but he told himself that the pace he set would have been brutal to even a skilled mountain man.

Unfortunately, he could do little to hide his tracks in the snow. He'd just have to move faster and ignore the burning of his lungs in the thin mountain air.

Breathing hard, Kirk checked his position again about thirty minutes later. He estimated that Pepper might soon catch Sara's scent. He removed Sara's sweater from the plastic bag and allowed Pepper a whiff before he signaled the dog to begin a back-and-forth route, hoping he hadn't tried too soon. If Sara hadn't survived, or if her scent was too faint, he could waste too much of the animal's stamina and strength. Pepper would run until she dropped, in hope of a successful rescue. Kirk had to make sure he didn't ask more of the animal than she was capable of giving.

As if their task wasn't difficult enough, the snow that had dwindled to occasional snowflakes for hours began to swell into another full-fledged storm. The only good thing was that the snow would quickly fill in his tracks.

Kirk neither saw nor heard any signs of another human being on the mountain. Yet, he sensed he was being pursued. If he found Sara alive, he would have to figure out a way to slip past whoever was after her and come down safely.

But that was a very big "if."

Pepper's ears rose, and she wagged her tail excitedly. She'd caught Sara's scent. She no longer zigzagged but headed almost straight upward, leading Kirk through a dense stand of pines, around boulders higher than his head and past a cave in the cliffs.

When Pepper stopped and growled, Kirk at first feared that she'd lost the scent with a wind change. But then he realized that Pepper had stopped because she could go no farther. They'd come up against a solid wall of ice.

And right beside them was half the airplane—the tail section. Even from here he could clearly see that no one was there. Taking out his binoculars, he searched the mountain for signs of the fuselage.

Buried in snow, about five hundred yards from the tail section, he could make out the flattened fuselage and the silhouette of the broken cockpit window. But no body. He'd have to check it out. She could be hidden on the other side or buried in the snow.

He stepped toward the aircraft, but Pepper blocked his path. Knowing her senses were much keener than his, he knelt, wishing, not for the first time, that she could speak to him with words. "What is it, girl?"

Pepper lightly took his gloved hand between her teeth and tugged him toward the cliff. She looked up and barked. Clearly, she wanted to go straight up the side of the mountain.

Kirk looked back at the crashed plane, flattened as if with a giant hammer. Without going closer, he already knew that if Sara had been in that plane when it crashed, she would be dead. But if the plane had smashed at a higher elevation and dumped her out before tumbling farther down the mountain, she could still be alive and above them, as Pepper seemed to indicate.

With someone in possible pursuit, Kirk didn't waste time. He believed in his dog. "Okay, girl. We're going up."

First, he hitched Pepper into her harness, which was attached to a sturdy rope. Once Kirk climbed up the cliff's face, he'd haul her up hand over hand. Pepper nudged him, quite impatient with his speed.

"Okay, okay. I'm going."

The climb wasn't quite straight up. Kirk told himself he'd overcome worse obstacles. But not in this kind of wind. Not after hours of trudging through hip-deep snow. Not when he couldn't see five feet in front of him. And certainly not when he presented a clear silhouette for a shooter.

But Pepper's determination gave him hope that Sara was up there waiting for him. And when he cleared the top, he smelled what Pepper had been so excited about.

Smoke.

Chapter Five

The fire had kept Sara and Abby warm enough to survive the night, and Sara had dozed between the tasks of putting additional wood on the fire and feeding Abby. She awakened groggy, startled by a noise she couldn't quite place.

She checked her watch. Half past ten. She hadn't meant to sleep so late, but with the blizzard outside still raging, there was no reason to get up and make the decision whether to stay here, head for higher ground with her cell phone, or try to walk out before she lost more of her strength. The lack of food and the cold had worn her down into a strange lethargy, although she was sure she'd kept up their core temperatures and avoided hypothermia and dehydration by her determined efforts. Not only had she kept the fire going, but inspiration made her heat stones in the fire and then place them around their extremities. That extra warmth had been worth the effort of gathering the stones and carrying them back, but she'd paid for the heat with depletion of her energy.

Lifting her arms was now an effort. She wasn't sure she could stand, but for Abby's sake, if she had to, she would crawl to the downed tree to collect more wood to keep the fire going another twenty-four hours. On stiff arms and knees, she moved out from her lair into hard-falling snow and wind that seemed to chill her straight to the bone.

The minute she stuck her nose out, a warm tongue swiped across her cheek and a dog's familiar whine greeted her ears.

"Pepper?" Sara had to be dreaming. Because where Pepper led, Kirk followed.

She didn't know whether to laugh or cry or question her sanity. And as much as she and Abby needed rescuing, Kirk was the last man on earth she wanted to face. The pain of the divorce was still too sharp.

A man's silhouette solidified out of the snow. He was wearing a dark blue parka and carrying a huge pack. She'd never thought to see Kirk again and had tried to bury her feelings along with her memories. The good recollections and the bad ones had haunted many a sleepless night. But looking at him now caused those dammed-up feelings to make her head spin, reminding her of her loss and all she'd missed since their split. She would not faint—even if her knees did feel like jelly. Now was no time for silly, emotional reactions—not with Abby's life at stake.

"Sara?"

She covered up both her relief and her pain with sarcasm. "Now I know what it takes to get you home—a plane crash."

"Are you all right?" He strode toward her, his concerned eyes searching her face; he was evaluating her condition like the professional he was.

"That would depend how you define 'all right.'"

His voice was gentle. "Any broken bones, internal or external bleeding?"

She shook her head, told herself to keep to the practical chores needed for survival. "Unless you have a way to get us out of here in this storm, I could use help gathering firewood and something to eat."

He shrugged off his huge pack, dipped his hand inside and pulled out a power bar. She held out her hand, forgetting that she'd taped a diaper around it to keep her fingers warm, and saw his brows rise in surprise.

He unwrapped the power bar and handed it to her. "Very innovative."

"You have no idea."

Pepper had stuck her head inside the makeshift igloo. Outside, her tail wagged ferociously.

"Dog," Abby said.

Kirk's gaze went to the snow shelter and then back to her. "The baby?"

Sara bit into the bar and chewed. Until now, she hadn't realized how very hungry she was. She'd been busy trying to keep warm and feed Abby, and the dual drain on her body had taken a toll. Now that Kirk had arrived, exhaustion took over, and she swayed on her feet.

"Abby's okay."

Kirk handed her his canteen and field-ration meal, the kind that heated automatically upon being opened. "Go eat. I'll gather more wood."

A million thoughts spun through her head but she pointed toward the downed tree. "There's a dead pine over there."

Kirk removed an ax from his gear, waited until she

crawled inside the shelter, then shoved his pack in after her. "Help yourself to whatever you need. But don't use the radio."

"Okay. Thanks." Sara forced herself to eat slowly instead of gobbling the turkey, stuffing and green beans, hoping the food would replenish her energy. Until Kirk had arrived, she'd been going on pure adrenaline, and she hadn't much left in reserve. Maybe that was good. Her emotions felt numbed.

After finishing every bite of the hot meal and washing it down with water from Kirk's canteen, Sara dug into his pack and found a set of snowpants, which she slipped on over her jeans. She donned an extra pair of thick socks and set aside the gloves for later.

Abby awakened, and Sara breast-fed her daughter. When the howling wind died around them and the temperature inside increased, Sara realized that Kirk had placed a tarp over the branches of her roof, leaving a hole in the center large enough for the smoke to exit.

She'd just finished changing Abby's diaper, when Kirk crawled into the snow hut and Pepper followed. The tiny shelter suddenly seemed crowded and warm. The food must have rejuvenated her because Sara's emotions spiked. For so long she'd wanted this moment of their family coming together to happen, but when it hadn't, she'd told herself that it was for the best. If Kirk didn't ever meet his daughter, he'd never ask for joint custody, and Sara wouldn't have to share Abby. Selfish of her? Yes. But sensible, too. Kirk had a simpatico relationship with his dogs, not with his ex-wife, or with his child. But then, he hadn't yet met Abby.

Abby should know her father. On one hand, however, Sara feared Kirk would reject their daughter. On the other, she was afraid he wouldn't.

Although Kirk stole several glances at the baby, he focused mostly on Sara. "You did great, you know."

"I had no choice."

"Most people wouldn't have lasted through last night's storm." He took up over half the room, but he scrunched up his knees to make space for Pepper as he fed the fire with wood. "Did you have matches to start the fire?"

Relief shot through her. She didn't have the strength to discuss Abby or their divorce. Not yet. Maybe Kirk sensed her mood, or maybe he didn't want to talk about their past either.

"When the pilot parachuted out of the plane, he grabbed my computer case. Filled with books, the weight probably felt right to him and he believed he'd stolen my work—and left us to die. But I'd slipped my laptop into the diaper bag I'd strapped behind Abby's car seat. I only had my computer and Abby's diapers. I got a spark out of the battery."

Kirk chuckled, and the pride in his eyes warmed her.

"Did I ever tell you that you have a beautiful mind?"

"I should have been smarter. More careful." Abby fussed in the car seat, and Sara picked up the baby, held her over her shoulder and rubbed her back to ease out a burp. "I know my program is valuable, but I never imagined that anyone would do more than maybe try to steal it."

"Your home was trashed, the hard drive of your desktop computer empty."

"I wiped the hard drive." Abby started to cry. Probably the gas in her tummy hurt. Poor little tyke. Although the literature she'd read claimed breast-fed babies didn't get as much gas as those bottle-fed, Abby almost always burped once after feeding, then again a few minutes later.

Pepper ignored the noisy baby and kept her eyes on Sara.

Kirk spoke louder to be heard over Abby's cries. "Where are your program's backups?"

"Hidden." At least she'd done something right. But then, she'd always protected her work. What she couldn't forgive herself for was putting her daughter's life at risk. As if in agreement, Abby began to scream and kick her feet.

"Can I hold her?" Kirk asked. From the tender but irritated look in his eyes, he obviously thought she wasn't comforting her daughter.

Maybe he was right. Abby certainly seemed to spend a large amount of time crying. Still, Sara knew she was a good mother. Her pediatrician agreed. Some babies were difficult. Abby was one of those, yet that had nothing to do with how much Sara loved her.

With a pang, Sara handed the baby to Kirk. In protest, Abby turned her head toward her mother and cried harder. Her tears seemed to say, *How could you do this to me?* Sara supposed she would have felt betrayed if the child had ceased crying the moment her daddy held her, so she couldn't stop a tiny hitch of satisfaction.

Kirk bounced the baby gently, seemingly fascinated by her tiny tears, her red, red face and her fists clenched so ferociously. Sara supposed she should warn him. But then she thought of the nine months of pregnancy that she'd spent alone. Bearing the pain of childbirth without her husband to hold her hand. Months of midnight feedings. He had just climbed a mountain during a blizzard to rescue them. For that she owed him. But when it came to Abby, she owed him nothing.

"Stop bouncing her, Kirk. She just ate."

He glanced from Abby to her breasts. "You still have enough milk?"

She nodded. At the mention of the intimate subject, she tried to appear casual but suspected he wasn't fooled. He knew every inch of Sara's body, knew what pleased her, knew what drove her wild. But that had been a long time ago, she reminded herself.

"How did you know I'm breast-feeding?"

He juggled Abby, ignoring Sara's warning. "Logan Kincaid told me when he hired me."

"Logan Kincaid?" The brilliant computer programmer who'd sold Sara part of her source code had told Kirk that she was breast-feeding?

Abby burped loudly, predictably spitting up on her daddy's shoulder. Sara chuckled and wagered with herself how long it would take him to hand the baby back to her. Five seconds? Ten? Twenty?

Kirk frowned and gently placed Abby in the crux of one arm, picked up a handful of snow and calmly rubbed away the sour milk. The smell would take hours to fade, but she said nothing, simply enjoyed watching him deal with the mishap. She'd forgotten how down-to-earth he could be. She should have figured that a man who worked next to bombs all day wouldn't get upset about a little baby spit.

"You knew she was going to do that, didn't you," he muttered, partly annoyed, partly amused. "I should have listened. I should have listened to you about a lot of things."

Refusing to let his reflections soften her feelings toward him even a smidgen, she put off the personal comments for a later discussion.

"What does Logan Kincaid have to do with me?"

"He found me at the ranch. He told me your plane had gone down."

Maybe she still hadn't recovered enough for her brain to work properly, but she couldn't make the connections necessary to understand what he was saying. "You aren't making sense. Why would Logan Kincaid find you?" Kirk had been stationed in Pakistan. "Or were you on leave at a ranch?"

"Logan runs a private corporation of ex-military and CIA types. They take on secret missions for the government. Within hours of your plane going down, Logan Kincaid knew a witness had seen a man parachute to safety. He also knew your house had been trashed."

"Someone wants my program."

"Badly enough to kill for it," he added, his tone hard, his eyes harder. "But who?"

Pepper responded to his tone by lifting her head. He petted her reassuringly and she snuggled against his legs.

"The program's worth a lot of money, so my competitors would be interested, of course." She paused, thinking. "Terrorists might want to stop our government from using my software. If it tests out, and it will, the program is so fast it can digitalize a face and identify it, even in poor lighting. Even if the person wears a hat or sunglasses. I've figured out how to—"

"Sara—"

His sharp tone made her realize she'd been about to delve into the technical intricacies of her work.

"—who else would kill for your program?"

"There're a few nutcases out there, people who believe their privacy will be violated." She shrugged. "But kill me to stop the government from installing my program in every airport in the country? I don't think so."

"Logan believes they will try again."

Oh God.

She'd been so busy surviving, she hadn't thought that far ahead. But since the thief hadn't gotten her program in the computer bag the pilot had stolen, and since they'd come up empty on the hard drive at her house, they might come looking for her computer on the crashed aircraft. When they didn't find her body or her computer, they'd know she had survived. And would try again.

Abby wasn't safe. Blood rushed from her face and she swayed, slightly faint.

Kirk reached out a hand to steady her. "Take it easy. You have lots of help. Logan's team are experts in—"

"How do you know you can trust him?" Her heart raced, and suddenly Kirk's arrival seemed too timely, too suspicious.

Breathe, she told herself. If Logan was a bad guy,

Kirk wasn't in on the deception. True blue to his core, he never lied, and it simply wasn't in him to make any choice except the right one. They may have had marital troubles, but she could always count on him when he finally showed up. Their problem had been the long absences combined with her worries over his dangerous missions. However, when he had been around, he was dependable, honest and caring. The kind of man who helped little old ladies across the street. The kind of man who would stay awake all night nursing a sick puppy. A hero. His expertise had saved many lives—his commanding officers had never failed to tell her about his accomplishments with pride.

But had Logan Kincaid conned Kirk?

"Excuse me?" Kirk looked at her as if she'd lost her mind. "Logan hired me to find you."

"Maybe *he* wants the program."

"I don't think so. His reputation is impeccable. And he works for our government."

Sara knew all too well how one arm of the government might not approve of what another arm was doing. But she didn't want to argue with Kirk, who believed in the chain of command, in following orders, in having faith in one's superiors.

"You checked Logan out?"

"I didn't have time. I was worried about you. And Abby." Kirk hesitated, and a glimmer of pain shone in his eyes before he looked away. "How come you never told me about her?"

"What?" She glared at him. She'd spent months hating him for rejecting his daughter, and now he claimed that he'd never known about Abby? Frustration and fury made her raise her voice. "Were you too busy to read my letters?"

"Your letters were the highlight of my days."

Maybe her close call with death made saying what she felt easier. Maybe she simply was worn down from her ordeal. She couldn't keep the pain from pouring out. Didn't try to rein in her sarcasm. "Yeah, you missed me so much that you came back to live with me."

He flinched and withdrew his hand from her shoulder. "I read every letter at least ten times. You know that."

She did know. He'd told her often how much the daily letters had meant to him, how he looked forward to hearing about her life, how her words kept them close when they weren't together. That's why she'd been so hurt when he had never responded. So she'd sent the divorce papers and he'd signed them, and that was the end of their marriage. However often she'd told herself that he was no longer a part of her life, he'd sneaked into her thoughts when she dropped her guard. Like when she'd been hanging upside down on the edge of the cliff. Like during the lonely nights when she remembered how good making love with him had been. Like when she saw his stubborn determination in the child they had made during his last leave. Dealing now with the issues between them sharpened the pain, but maybe once they cleared the air, she could let go of her past and go on with her life.

"I wrote you about Abby twice."

"I didn't get anything about Abby."

"When you didn't answer—"

"I didn't get them," he insisted, in a voice that reminded her of a soft sheath housing the sharpest of blades.

"—I figured you didn't care." She finished in a rush, wondering if he could ever know how many hours she'd spent wondering why she hadn't heard from him.

"You know better." His eyes flashed anger at her assumption. "When did you send the letters?"

"Right after your last leave."

Right after the condom they'd been using had broken. She hadn't been in her fertile time of the month, so she had figured she was safe. She'd figured wrong. And had been so happy about the baby, and scared and thrilled to have her at the same time.

He'd never gotten her letters?

She'd spent months resenting him for avoiding his responsibilities. Months feeling hurt that he'd rejected their baby.

"I was in Kuwait. Your letters might have been blown up during the embassy bombing. I should have guessed a few had gone missing, but you weren't writing regularly then." Kirk's voice was choked. "And then the divorce papers came and, soon after that, Gabby got killed."

"I'm sorry." She'd heard about Gabby's death through the military grapevine. Knew that the two men had been as close as brothers. They'd trained the animals together, put their lives on the line for one another. She hadn't known Gabby that well, but what she'd known of the man, she'd liked and respected.

"I resigned my commission, Sara."

She couldn't have been more shocked if he'd told

her he had suddenly taken up knitting. The U.S. Marine Corps had been such a large part of his life for so long that she had difficulty wrapping her mind around his statement. She almost asked why, and then decided she didn't want to be that much of a masochist. He hadn't quit for her. She'd made her feelings about their interminable separations known to him long before she'd accidentally gotten pregnant during his last leave. She'd wanted him to resign. And he had. But he hadn't done it for *her* or to keep their marriage together, and that hurt enough to make her turn away from him.

But in the small space of the snow hut, she couldn't avoid him any more than she could keep back her emotions. She tried a different tack. "What do you do now?"

"I train dogs for other handlers."

"Drug and bomb sniffers?" She'd named the two most dangerous occupations for dogs and their handlers.

"I'm training the animals, not going on missions."

"But—"

"I only agreed to take this mission after Logan told me that it was you."

He looked so sincere, as if he believed what he'd just told her. She couldn't allow herself any hope. "You'll re-up when you get done grieving for Gabby."

"I won't." She could tell that he knew she didn't believe him.

He hesitated slightly, but remained honest as always. "Logan Kincaid has offered me a job with the

Shey Group, but I haven't yet decided whether to accept his offer.''

"I see." So maybe he wouldn't rejoin the military, but if he worked for the Shey Group, he'd still be working in considerable danger. As far as she could see, nothing much had changed.

"I missed you, Abby. I was hoping you might give us another chance."

"I can't."

"And I wanted to see my daughter."

"Thanks." Again she covered her pain with sarcasm. Most men would have been annoyed and left her to stew in an angry silence, but Kirk knew her too damn well. He knew she used a cutting tongue to hide her feelings, and he always reacted calmly, so she added, "And it's *our* daughter."

"She's stopped crying." Kirk grinned. "I think she likes me."

Abby tugged on the metal tag of his pocket sleeve. Her tiny fingers couldn't quite grasp the metal and when they did, she invariably lost her grip.

"She cries when she's hungry, tired or hurting. Or when she wants attention."

"What a sensible girl you are."

At Kirk's attention, Abby blossomed, her round cheeks dimpling with a winsome smile. She spoke in a baby voice, "Good girl."

"You're already talking?" He glanced from Abby to Sara and back again. "Are you brilliant like your mom?"

His statement made Sara uncomfortable. She'd spent too many years of her childhood being called The Brain to want her daughter to be made fun of like that. "Her vocabulary consists of *mama, good girl, dog, cat, ball, eat* and *up*. Pepper probably knows more words."

Kirk shot her one of those piercing, perceptive looks. "You going to argue with everything I say?"

"Maybe." She scowled at him, knowing she needed to keep her anger as a barrier against the pain of seeing him again. Already she had the urge to set aside their differences and forgive him for being the man he was. And it would be the second biggest mistake of her life. She already knew that he never put his family first. He'd made that agonizingly clear. She couldn't fall under his spell again.

Sara didn't like to make the same mistake twice. And Kirk was what he was. A very kind and tender man with a very large heart—with too much room in it. Sara hadn't wanted to be just one of the people he included in his world; she'd wanted to be his whole world—or, at least, enough of it that she could count on their living together.

And she definitely didn't want Abby to become attached to a man who would almost certainly break her heart. Kirk would leave again. As soon as he finished grieving for Gabby, he would re-up, and the Marine Corps would welcome him back like a lost family member who'd come home after a difficult journey.

Sara had to keep her emotional distance. Kirk was simply too accustomed to handling her; she couldn't allow him to get close again. Older and wiser since their split, she refused to fall for those tender looks at Abby. She needed to keep in mind that he would leave them again—whether he knew it yet or not.

She didn't care how bitchy or ungrateful she sounded. Until they got off this mountain, they would be eating and sleeping in such close quarters that avoiding him would be impossible. If her only defense was her memories of their separations and a sharp tongue, then she'd use the weapons at hand.

"Dada." Kirk patted his chest and tried to get Abby to repeat the words. "Dada."

Abby stuck her fingers in her mouth. Gently, he pulled them out. "Say 'Dada' for me, little girl."

"Good girl?"

"Yes, you're a very good girl." He grinned at her. "Now say 'Dada'."

Abby stuck her fingers back in her mouth and ignored him. *Smart girl,* Sara thought. *Don't fall for that sweet charm like your mother did.*

Chapter Six

Since Logan had told him about Sara's plane crash, Kirk had kept his emotions locked down tight. He'd gone into his mission mode—analyzing, assessing, calculating the odds—a mode he'd found useful during dangerous missions where keeping his emotions in check might make the difference between survival and death—not just for him, but for anyone in or near the buildings where he searched for bombs.

Deep in his heart, he'd never believed Sara and Abby had died. Hope had kept him going. Hope had kept him from losing it after he saw the crashed plane. Hope had had him scaling that cliff in a blizzard. And hope kept back the despair now.

Since he'd found them alive, in better shape than he could have thought possible, feelings had bombarded him in giant blasts that rocked him to the core. Joy over Sara and Abby's safety alternated with worry over getting them off the mountain. Just seeing Sara again brought him a kind of peace. Hearing her sharp tongue was better than the silence of his own thoughts over these past horrible months without her. During his last leave, Sara had asked him to quit the military—and he'd refused. But he'd always felt guilty that he hadn't given her fears more consideration. He'd signed the divorce papers, giving Sara what she'd wanted, still hoping that he could someday change her mind, but obligated to complete his military hitch.

Then Gabby died—his best friend, his partner. And while Kirk had grieved, he'd thrown himself into work, determined to help root out the terrorists who had planted the bomb that had killed Gabby. Success had eased some of the pain he'd felt over his friend's death, but hard work brought no relief from the loss of his marriage. Without Sara behind him to give his days meaning, the job he'd loved had become just work. His zest and enthusiasm were gone. Sara was no longer waiting for him to come home. She refused to answer his phone calls. So he'd leased his ranch and simply thrown himself into his day-to-day tasks, unable to think about his future.

"Are you dead?" He could still hear his partner, Gabby, prodding him as Kirk procrastinated over signing the divorce papers. "It ain't over until you're dead."

And Kirk was very much alive. Alive enough to feel the pain of rejection and remorse. But his heart was still beating, his thoughts racing.

Maybe he *could* change Sara's mind, but she was the most stubborn woman he'd ever known. She rarely made quick decisions, but pondered over the possibilities until she convinced herself she'd made the correct choice. And once she decided, she seldom wavered. She obviously didn't want him back in her life, not that she could argue while they remained trapped by the storm on the mountain. To give him a measly glimmer of hope, he'd seen several sparks of the old Sara, a few moments when she hadn't completely hidden her feelings from him. All her thoughts of him couldn't be bad—she was too reasonable a person not to remember the good times in their marriage, too.

He had to make the most of this opportunity, but how? Kirk glanced at his daughter in the crook of his arm and his heart swelled with pride and joy. And more guilt. He should have been at Sara's side during Abby's birth. He'd missed the first eight months of Abby's life. As a baby, she couldn't possibly know she was supposed to have a daddy to look after her, but soon she would be walking and talking and asking questions. Children needed their fathers.

Yet Kirk didn't believe he could convince Sara to take him back for the sake of their daughter. He'd hurt Sara by refusing to quit the Marines. She believed he'd put the needs of his country before their marriage. And he had. More guilt stabbed him, especially when he knew that if he had to make the same decision again, he'd choose Sara first and foremost. He'd learned too late that what they'd had together was rare and precious and that he should have fought much harder to keep her. She was his life, his heart—and he'd lost her.

Sara had already heard his explanation. The CIA had gotten wind of a rumor that the Embassy in Pakistan would be bombed. They didn't know when the attack might come or from where. Since Kirk and Gabby were the best handlers in that hemisphere, their mission was to keep the American Embassy in Pakistan safe. Days had stretched into weeks, then months, before the attack finally came—a bomb smuggled inside the embassy. In doing his job, Gabby had sacrificed his life. Kirk had sacrificed his marriage.

Sara hadn't believed that waiting for the mission's completion was an option. She'd told him that after the danger in Pakistan ended, the military would send him to the next hot spot. Because Kirk knew he was good at what he did, he couldn't disagree with her assumption.

But he had to try.

Kirk had never backed down from dangerous or difficult missions. He wouldn't back down now. She hadn't believed him when he told her that he had no intention of rejoining the Marine Corps. He'd seen the disbelief in her eyes. And he'd realized that he'd hurt her so badly that she was protecting herself. Words weren't going to convince her. Actions might. If he had enough time... But time was the one thing he didn't have. They should be off the mountain tomorrow. And then she would leave him.

So he had to make the most of this opportunity together. That left him mere hours. Still, he'd go slowly. Sara reminded him of a wounded animal who didn't trust strangers. That he had caused her wounds sliced him up inside. While he wanted her to heal and didn't want to cause more damage, he couldn't let her go. He loved her too much. So, he had to make this effort or he'd never forgive himself.

Kirk and Sara took turns feeding the fire, and as the silence between them lengthened, the air crackled with tension. Motherhood hadn't changed Sara. She still had those model-high cheekbones, fine lips that had once responded so eagerly to his, and a graceful neck that he loved to plant kisses on or knead after she'd spent too many hours at her computer. They'd shared so many good times, and now Sara refused to say anything—and he didn't know where to start.

He couldn't speak to her about what was in his heart because she wasn't ready to listen. Instead, he stuck to the basics. "We won't have to walk all the way down the mountain. Just to a clearing about a mile away. When the wind dies down, a chopper will land and fly us out."

She nodded, staring into the fire, avoiding his gaze.

He tried again. "Are you warm enough? Want anything else to eat?"

"No, thanks."

Damn, she could be uncooperative. Words weren't going to break through her shell. He placed a hand on her ankle. "Sara."

She jerked her foot away, her eyes a bit wild. "What?"

"Do you hate me?" he forced himself to ask, surprised at how violently she'd reacted to a touch through snowpants, jeans and two layers of socks.

She didn't answer for so long that he wondered if she was back to ignoring him. But the tension that started in her jaw and ran down her stiff neck and rigid spine clued him in to the fact that she was thinking about his question. That she had to ponder for so long shook him, and when she finally lifted her gaze from the flames and let him see her pain, he went berserk inside.

She finally had her answer ready. And he already knew he didn't want to hear it.

The fire was reflected in her eyes, and the flames emphasized the hollows of her cheekbones, the fullness of her mouth. She'd always had the most adorable mouth, and it always spoke the truth. Sara didn't play games. A straight-shooter, she rarely even told a white lie.

The anguish in her words scorched him. ''I hate that our marriage meant so little to you that you threw it away. I hate that *I* meant so little to you that you left me wondering what I'd done wrong.''

''Oh, Sara.'' He groaned at the depth of her pain.

''I hate failing. I hate making mistakes and, except for sweet Abby, being with you was the biggest mistake of my life. I hate feeling that if I'd been more accepting—''

''It wasn't your fault.''

''Or if I had worked less—''

''Don't do this to yourself.''

''Or if I'd found a way to stay at your side.''

''In Pakistan? In Kuwait? While you were pregnant? It was too dangerous and you would have been miserable.''

She looked him straight in the eyes. ''I was miserable without you, but I'm over you now. I don't ever want to go back to that place.''

She was shutting him out, and he hadn't a clue what to say to convince her otherwise—especially when everything she said was true. He'd been a Marine for eight years. The first four, when she'd traveled with him, had been the best years of his life. But when the missions became too dangerous, civilians weren't allowed to accompany their spouses. Sara couldn't visit combat zones, and his long absences had put more stress on her than she could take.

"Are you seeing someone else?" he forced himself to ask. The thought of another man holding Sara and raising his daughter cut unbearably deep.

"You have no right to ask me that question." Her words weren't so much defiant as bleak. Sara sighed and closed her eyes, and her voice dropped to a whisper. "But, no, I'm not seeing anyone."

"We could—"

The sound of a chopper cut off his statement. After gently placing the sleeping Abby in her carrier, he backed out of the snow hut, stood and held his binoculars to his eyes to search the snow-filled sky.

Under the canopy of tree branches and hard-falling snow, they and the smoke from their campfire were effectively hidden from the chopper. But why was it up there, when Kirk had yet to send the signal to Logan?

Sara stepped beside him. "I strapped Abby into the carrier so even if she wakes up, she'll be safe from the fire— What's wrong?"

"I'm not sure anything is wrong. Logan instructed me to keep radio silence, but if he was sending the chopper up, I'd have figured he'd send a message first."

"Could mountains block the radio signal like they do my cell phone?"

He shook his head. "The radios don't require a satellite to work, but go by line of sight."

"Could the radio be broken?"

"It's unlikely. And there's no way to test it without

breaking silence." He frowned at the sky and put away the binoculars. "Are you up for a short hike? I want to move camp."

"It's almost dark. It's snowing. We have a protected hut and firewood. And you want to move because...?"

"You've been here too long. The chopper might have spotted your smoke."

"In all this snow?"

"They have thermal imagers. With the right equipment, the chopper could have spotted us."

"But don't we *want* it to spot us? Don't we want to be rescued?"

"Suppose someone else is looking for us in this storm? The same someone who trashed your apartment? The same someone who crashed your plane?"

Sara crossed her arms over her chest. "If your intent is to scare me, it's working."

He heard the chopper circling, turning back. "We're moving out. Get Abby."

From their shelter, Kirk yanked off the tarp that had served as their roof and folded it into his pack. Sara bundled up the baby in the extra clothing he'd brought and placed her in the sling that she wore on her back. Her computer dangled from her hand, and he took it from her.

"You'll need both hands free if you fall."

At least she trusted him with her precious computer. She didn't say a word as he placed it into his pack. They put out the fire and broke camp in less than three minutes.

Kirk signaled Pepper to stay close, and the animal obediently remained at their sides. However, she kept looking in the direction of the helicopter, and Kirk suspected her sensitive ears could still hear the engines.

Sara's face was grim, her lips tight and determined. "What about Abby's carrier?"

"It's too heavy and awkward to carry."

"But it protects her from the cold. She can't sleep on the ground. And holding her is impossible."

"Why?"

"She wriggles."

"She can sleep on my chest." At the doubt he saw on Sara's face, he reconsidered. "Maybe I can come back for the carrier."

Pepper let out a soft *woof,* her way of telling him the chopper had gotten louder and possibly turned around.

"Let's move out."

"I hope you know what you're doing," Sara muttered.

"So do I." Kirk patted her shoulder, pleased that this time she didn't jerk away. And then he grinned. "But I'm the best damn search and rescue man on the mountain."

Sara rolled her eyes and, if she didn't smile, her mouth softened at his attempt at humor. "You're the *only* search and rescue man on the mountain."

WITH A CONTENTED ABBY on her back, Sara trudged behind Kirk through the snow. Her daughter hadn't protested the mask Kirk had brought for her that kept her face warm and left openings for the eyes, nose and mouth. And she enjoyed the backpack, sitting quietly without complaining. Sara found the load heavy, but manageable, especially after glancing at Kirk's huge pack.

He walked steadily in front of her, breaking trail, holding back branches so they wouldn't catch her in the face and helping her over the rough and icy patches. Within five minutes of leaving the snow hut, she was totally lost and feeling dependent on Kirk. A feeling she hated. She didn't want to owe him anything. She didn't want to depend on him. But what choice did she have? She couldn't have picked a better man with whom to face the storm. His skills would keep them alive, and she never doubted his loyalty or honesty as she would have a stranger's.

But that special connection that she still felt between them concerned her. When he'd placed his hand on her ankle, she'd wanted him to do so much more. Afraid he'd see the need in her eyes and sense the loneliness inside, she'd overreacted to his touch, revealing more than she'd intended.

She reminded herself that he would have taken the same risks for strangers. He'd done so, many times. She had to fight to keep him at an emotional distance, which wasn't easy considering their desperate circumstances. Still, she had to try.

It was difficult to forget all they had shared. His last leave had been so bittersweet. The last time they'd made love. And had created Abby.

Sara had no way to judge time, except that with every passing hour the white snow turned to gray and the cold grew more bitter. Without the mittens, woolen face mask, snowpants and thermal underwear Kirk had brought her, she would have been frostbitten by now. As it was, she still felt chilled. Not even keeping to his tough pace could warm her.

Abby, in the pack, didn't have the luxury of movement. But Kirk had wrapped an additional blanket around the baby and he stopped periodically to check her fingers and toes. During the last check, he'd promised to stop soon. But apparently he hadn't found the right cover.

"We're almost there," he told her, his voice muffled by the wind.

She had followed him straight into the cave before she realized that he'd found the perfect shelter. While the roof was tall enough for her to stand, Kirk stooped to avoid hitting his head. She gazed uneasily into the black depths.

"What about bears?"

Taking out his flashlight, he shone it into the interior. "None in here." He slid off his pack and dumped it on the cave floor. "There are matches in a case. If you gather some kindling, I'll bring back some heavier wood."

"First, I need to feed Abby."

He nodded and ducked back outside. Sara winced as the cold air bit into her chest, and she wrapped a blanket around both the child and herself. Hungry, Abby sucked hard and swallowed quickly. Her eagerness and strength reassured Sara. She'd feared taking her daughter into the storm, but Abby seemed no worse for the time spent outside. Her rosy cheeks glowed with health and her body, nestled against Sara's, was warm and cuddly.

Sara had decided to breast-feed because she'd read how healthy it was for the baby. She'd never expected to enjoy the experience. But feeding her child this way, holding her skin to skin, brought a closeness and a bonding that she'd never anticipated. She hadn't known so much love was in her. Hadn't known she could take so much joy in Abby's smiles or in her well-being.

And until now, she hadn't known how much she'd wanted to share that joy over her precious child with Kirk. No one else would ever take such pleasure in each new word Abby learned, in her tiny smiles, in her swift adaptability to changing circumstances.

Sara had just finished changing Abby's diaper when Kirk returned with an armload of wood. He didn't complain that she hadn't started making the fire, just dumped the wood and set about gathering kindling himself.

Abby wanted to explore and seemed set on crawling. Sara floated the blanket over the hard-packed dirt and set the baby down. Full of curiosity, Abby raised herself to hands and knees and took off to investigate her new world.

Kirk dug out matches from his pack and glanced at the crawling baby with a frown. "Are you tired of holding her?"

"She needs exercise. She hasn't crawled around since the crash."

Abby reached the edge of the blanket, picked up a stick and tried to jam it in her mouth. Sara plucked the stick from her hand. "I don't have her pacifier."

Kirk dug into his pack and handed her a plastic baby bottle with a nipple attached. "Maybe she can chew on this."

Since he'd known from the start of his journey that

she was breast-feeding, he must have brought the bottle in case the child had survived and she hadn't. But, of course, Kirk didn't say so, and she wondered what else he might be protecting them from that she couldn't even imagine.

Pepper settled on the edge of the blanket, as if guarding the baby. Sara gathered leaves and twigs into a pile a few feet away from the blanket and near the entrance. The cave was roomier than the snow hut and the walls blocked the wind better. However, they would require a larger fire to heat the larger area, and that meant more wood.

Sara stood, prepared to do her part. "If you'll keep an eye on Abby, I'll go for more firewood."

"Not necessary. There's a stack outside the cave. But you could gather some clean snow in this pot to melt."

Sara realized that to give her privacy while feeding the baby, he hadn't brought in the wood. At his consideration, her heart softened toward him.

Don't make the same mistake. He might be taking great care of them now, but he'd soon be back at the job he loved—maybe with Logan's team, and if not with the Shey Group, then with someone else. In fact, if she hadn't been in danger, he wouldn't have been with them at all. She recalled the way he'd said he missed her, the heat in his eyes that told her he wanted to try again, but she dismissed his feelings. Gabby's death and Abby's birth may have thrown him, but when he finished his grieving and his celebrating he would return to doing what he'd always done, protecting the lives of others by risking his own.

At first, she'd wanted him to quit the Marines because he wished to be with her. She had kept hoping he'd miss her enough to do something on his own about their separations—without her prodding. Because if she'd asked him to stop, and he did so because of her, he'd grow to resent her. But he'd kept on, and clearly expected her to do the same. She'd finally come right out and asked him to quit, and he'd refused. So she'd sent the divorce papers. Maybe to others the gesture seemed cold, but she just hadn't had the strength or the courage to make the phone call—especially after he'd hurt her so badly by never answering her letters about their daughter. A nice, clean, fast break had been for the best.

Only now, they were together again. While they'd been apart it hadn't been easy preventing him from invading her thoughts. But she'd managed. Over the past months she'd gotten better at keeping her mind occupied with work and Abby. Now he was here. Alive. Protective. So kind she wanted to slap him for making her remember how good they'd been together.

Damn him.

Efficiently, he lit the fire using the dried leaves, then coaxed the twigs to catch before adding thicker pieces of wood. His large hands, his fingers dexterous, fed the fire with smooth precision. She remembered those same hands on her. She thought about a midnight swim in Panama that had ended with them making love in the moonlight, and a romantic Valentine's Day, a tub filled with rose petals and a very naked, very charming Kirk surrounded by lighted candles. Sara didn't want to remember, but how could she forget, with his every movement bringing back the memories?

Abby chewed on the bottle's nipple, and Pepper settled down with her head on her paws, her watchful gaze on the baby.

When Sara neared the entrance, she saw that Kirk had draped the tarp over most of the opening, leaving a hole at the top to draw out the smoke. In minutes, he had the fire burning hot enough to add some much thicker branches.

"Keep an eye on Abby." Sara suspected her request was unnecessary. Between the dog and Kirk, Abby would be well cared for.

Sara stepped outside, as much to escape Kirk and her memories as to gather snow. She scooped clean snow into the pot to melt for drinking water. The wind had picked up again and more snow had fallen, enough to almost cover their footprints. She couldn't see any stars, didn't glance but once at the sky. She tucked her head down to keep the snow out of her eyes. The frigid temperature had dropped enough to make her hurry back inside.

Abby had crawled over to Pepper. She had two fistfuls of fur and was trying to pull herself to her feet. Pepper didn't seem to mind.

Sara handed the snow-filled pot to Kirk. "What's for dinner?"

"Steak and peppers, or chili. Your choice."

"Either one sounds good. I'm starved."

"Up." Abby pulled herself to her feet for a second, then plopped onto her bottom. She giggled, re-grabbed Pepper's fur and started the entire process all over again.

Kirk handed Sara a food packet. It took only minutes to heat, and she dug into the steak and peppers with appreciation. After a few bites, she noticed that Kirk had yet to take out a meal for himself. "Aren't you eating?"

"I'm not hungry."

That had to be a lie. She hadn't seen him eat anything since he'd arrived. Between climbing the mountain and carrying his pack, he'd burned plenty of energy. She'd gone through the top portion of his pack. They had at least four or five more meals in there.

She frowned at him. "Are you conserving our supplies?"

"I'm not hungry."

"Don't patronize me. I thought we're getting off this mountain tomorrow."

"We are." She stared at him until he added, "If the weather breaks."

"I'm not going to eat alone."

Stubbornly, he turned his back to her and pulled out a cup and a packet of instant coffee. "Yes, you are. You missed several meals and need extra calories to feed Abby."

"And we need you strong to get us out of here. Hungry men do not make good decisions." She went to his pack, tossed him a packet of food. "Eat."

He shook his head, grinned and accepted the food. "When I was missing you, I forgot how bossy you are."

When I was missing you. He'd said the words with such simplicity that she recognized that he *had* missed her. Of course he'd missed her. She'd doubted many things, but never his love for her. And for the first time she realized that she hadn't been the only one hurt by their divorce.

He handed her the coffee cup and their fingers touched. His hands were warm and strong, and she had to resist taking a seat beside him, leaning into him to share his strength. She no longer had that right. And although she sensed he would welcome the closeness, she didn't want to become accustomed again to his touch, or his masculine scent, or the sheer pleasure of knowing she wasn't alone. Experience told her that the closer she allowed herself to get to him, the more she'd suffer when he left.

He spoke between bites of food. "Logan said you live in a house?"

"I moved into my grandmother's home. After Abby was born, I wanted to put down roots." She sipped the coffee and appreciated the warmth as well as the flavor. Since there was only one cup, they would have to share—another intimacy she couldn't avoid. Careful not to spill any of the hot liquid, she handed him back his cup.

His eyes twinkled. "Do you have a garden?"

She was always trying to grow things: flowers, vegetables—fruits when they'd lived in Panama. But she simply didn't have a green thumb. Her plants didn't die, they just didn't flourish. Kirk used to tease her that she didn't talk to them in the right way. He'd claimed that plants needed more than computer programming words to blossom.

"I plan to start a garden this summer. I want to feed Abby fresh vegetables."

"Uh-huh." He restrained a smile, sipped the coffee

and handed back the cup. "If you sell your software for big bucks, you can afford to hire a gardener."

"Maybe I will." But she wouldn't. She wanted to do the work herself. After spending so many hours in front of her computer, she liked an excuse to go outside. The fresh air and exercise helped clear her mind.

"Sara."

"Hmm?"

"How many people know about your program?"

She knew why he'd asked the question. Sara had never liked working as an employee at a large corporation. Although the steady paycheck was nice, the drawbacks were many. The major one being that any work she developed even on her own time still belonged to the corporation. So she'd quit and started her own business. She was the sole owner of her business, and not many others were aware of her private work into face-recognition programs. Only people who knew about her work could come after it—but how many had the resources to do so with such viciousness?

"On the government side, I just don't know." Sara finished her food and washed it down with more coffee. "Several corporations were working on projects similar to mine, and I know of two independents who are about a year or two behind me. One tried to buy me out several years ago. Another competitor suggested we work together, but I wasn't interested."

"Maybe one of them wants to catch up in a hurry by stealing your program."

"Last week, I would have told you that you had to be mistaken."

But last week she hadn't been in a plane that crashed on a mountain during a blizzard.

Chapter Seven

Kirk might have been hoping for a sleeping baby and a romantic night alone with Sara by the fire, but he didn't get it. All thoughts of stealing a kiss evaporated with the baby's restless crying.

They spent a long, sleepless night in the cave. Sara had been right about Abby; the baby didn't like Kirk holding her while she slept. She'd been so cranky that Kirk had considered retracing his steps in the dark to retrieve the carrier for the baby to sleep in, but he didn't want to leave Sara alone.

Kirk couldn't put out of his mind, either, the firing of that stray gunshot during his climb, nor the whir of the chopper that shouldn't have been searching for them during the storm. Jack Donovan might fly the chopper by the seat of his pants, but he was clearly ex-military and obeyed orders. And Logan was waiting for Kirk to send a radio signal. He feared they weren't alone on the mountain. So, as much as they all needed rest, it was better to miss a little sleep than to leave Sara and Abby in danger.

Abby didn't fall asleep until the next morning during the hike down the mountain. After fussing through the night while they sang softly and rocked her, she'd finally fallen into an exhausted sleep on Sara's back.

The weather hadn't really cleared, although the snowfall had let up. They'd seen no sign of the sun. Instead, a flat grayness blanketed the slope, making the walking treacherous and judging distances difficult. Kirk led them carefully down the slope as gusts of wind howled through the trees, occasionally hurling sharp icicles at them, or shooting stinging flurries of snow into their faces.

He stopped at frequent intervals to listen, giving Sara an opportunity to rest and drink. She hadn't complained, but he could see the fatigue in her eyes and in her drooping posture. Much more accustomed to marathon sessions in front of her computer than walking in the outdoors, Sara kept her pace slow, but steady.

He handed her his canteen. "You okay?"

"I've been better." She glanced over her shoulder at the sleeping baby. "If we let her sleep, she's going to be up all night again."

"Don't wake her."

She looked at him searchingly. "Expecting trouble?"

He hesitated.

"I need to know the truth," she prodded between sips.

"We probably aren't alone on this mountain, and the other guys may be hostile."

"Oh." She swallowed hard, twisted the canteen's cap back on and handed it to Kirk with a brave nod.

"If they're going to attack us, they'll try to do it during extraction."

"How do you know?"

Because if he were the hunter, that's when he'd do it. "Because that's when we're most vulnerable and distracted."

"So how do we not become vulnerable and distracted?"

Kirk almost smiled at her straightforward question. To Sara, every problem had a solution. The key was asking the right questions. However, her world of computer programming tended to be more predictable than an unseen enemy about to close in from any number of directions.

"I want to delay sending the radio signal to Logan for the pickup," he told her.

"Why?"

Another woman might have complained of the cold and the snow. Sara always had to know the reasons for his decisions before she made up her own mind. And as much as he was in charge of their current safety, she would insist on participating fully in the decision making.

"I want to check out the clearing, make sure it's safe and secure before I give away our location."

"To make sure no one is there?"

He nodded. No point in telling her that the landing site could be booby-trapped and their enemy already miles away. Before she and the baby set one foot inside that clearing, he and Pepper would thoroughly check the ground.

"And what are we supposed to do while—"

"I'll find you a place to rest, out of the wind."

She shook her head, her eyes narrowing. "Separating is not a good idea."

"I've wanted to tell you that since you sent me those divorce papers," he teased her, deliberately misunderstanding her words.

"Don't joke about our failure," she snapped.

Abby stirred, her eyelids fluttering before she fell back into a sleep. Pepper cocked her head as if wondering at the sudden bickering.

"Sorry."

Sara was so touchy about the divorce that she obviously still found the subject as painful as he did. The problem was that she clearly wanted to go forward—alone. While he wanted to reclaim what they'd once had.

Didn't she see that this time the military wouldn't come between them? He'd resigned. For good.

Sara glanced around, trepidation in her eyes. "If you leave us, can I have the gun?"

Here he was thinking about the two of them getting back together, and Sara was thinking about survival. The role reversal jarred him back to reality. He forced himself to consider her idea.

"You don't know how to shoot—"

"Yes. I do."

"Really?" He reached into his pack, made sure the gun was on safety, then handed it to her. He expected her to cringe under the weight. But without hesitation she smoothly pulled the gun from the holster, checked the safety, expertly removed the clip and checked the load before ramming the clip home and easing off the safety. She'd had training. At no time did she point the gun at him, herself or Pepper, showing she'd also learned safety precautions well.

Sara, hater of all things military, had learned to shoot a gun. The contradiction confounded him. He stared at her as she sighted down the barrel with ease, wondering if he really knew her as well as he'd thought.

"Do you have a silencer?" she asked.

He placed a hand over hers, flicked the safety back on and took back the weapon. He didn't need to see her shoot to know that she could. Her weapon handling alone had revealed new skills, new determination. While on the one hand he was proud of her, his heart pinged with the regret that she expected to protect herself now. She no longer thought that she needed him.

As if sensing his confusion, she explained. "As a single mother I wanted to be able to defend myself and Abby, so I bought a gun and learned how to use it."

Another man might not have noticed her quiet hesitation, but Kirk had known Sara a long time. She had left out a vital element of her story. Not exactly a lie, but an omission.

"You got pregnant and, out of the blue, you decided you needed to defend yourself?" he asked skeptically.

"Our house was burglarized," she admitted. "Even after I put in an alarm system, they still broke in."

So why had she just hesitated? "Why didn't you want to tell me?"

She looked him square in the eyes. "I don't want you thinking that I can't look out for Abby."

"And that worries you?"

Sara nodded, her expression fierce and protective. "I won't have you thinking that you can take better care of Abby than I can."

"What are you saying?"

"I'm not interested in sharing custody."

"Sara." He placed a hand on her shoulder, his blood rushing in his ears as he fought to throttle back his anger. "Did you ever think that Abby might want to spend time with me?"

"She's not old enough to know you exist." Sara's tone might be clipped, but he saw the fear she was trying so hard to hide. And her fears contradicted one another. No way could he return to the military and at the same time take a baby with him. But not all fears were rational—not even Sara's.

He gentled his tone. "Didn't you think that I might want to spend time with her?"

"You never answered my letters telling you about my pregnancy, so I just assumed that you didn't have any feelings one way or another."

"But now you know differently."

"Besides, I'm breast-feeding. I couldn't exactly wrap her up and send her to you for a weekend visit."

He suspected Abby could drink formula from a bottle, but that wasn't really the issue. "I could have visited."

"And then she'd get to know you. You'd bond, and then leave on a mission. I don't want to put Abby through that kind of pain and I don't want to deal with the fallout. I don't want you to have anything to do with Abby.''

He realized Sara was so thoroughly convinced about his future that she couldn't even consider that he really had changed. ''Sara, I'm not going back—not even if the military offers me the position of head of worldwide operations for canine rescue. I'm ready to move on.''

''To the job Logan Kincaid offered you?''

''That's rescue work and not as dangerous. And I haven't yet decided to take his offer.'' Trying to defuse the emotional moment, Kirk started walking down the mountain again. ''I'd like for you both to come visit my ranch.''

Sara followed, but she didn't say anything for a long time.

They strode through a thick stand of pines, the snow hip-deep in places. In other spots, the ground resembled sheets of ice dimpled by rocks. Kirk didn't see many signs of animal life. Not even fresh tracks in the snow. These mountain creatures had the good sense to stay holed up in weather this cold.

Finally, from behind him, Sara spoke softly. ''Tell me about your ranch, Kirk. Did you buy the land?''

Was her attitude finally easing toward him? Had it been smart not to push her about Abby's custody? Or mention paying child support?

''The cabin is just one room, but it's all I need,'' he told her. ''Someday, I plan to build a proper house. But the land is fine for training the dogs. I have an obstacle course almost set up, pens, a barn for bad weather and enough acreage for the animals to roam.''

"Sounds like a good start."

"It's more than a start, Sara. It's my home now." When she didn't say more, he added, "You'd like the solitude. Deanna and Trey Marks are the closest neighbors. He raises some kind of timber crop."

"You're making civilian friends and putting down roots, are you?" she teased. While he socialized easily, she was a natural loner and had never understood why he liked to make new friends with small talk.

He neglected to mention that town was several hours away from his property. "Bumped into the neighbors at the butcher's while buying bones for the dogs."

He glanced ahead. Saw tracks in the snow. "Shh." He spun around so fast that she stopped talking in mid-sentence.

Pepper hadn't warned him of anyone's scent, so whoever had made the tracks must be long gone. But the shepherd could still be surprised by a person downwind of them.

Kirk didn't take any chances. He whispered "Stay here" to Sara, then headed about fifty yards toward the tracks. When he stopped to study the footprints, Sara edged up next to him.

He sighed. "I thought I told you to stay."

"I'm not a dog."

"Of course not. My dogs behave better."

"Your dogs give you blind obedience." She stared at the footprints. "One man?"

"Yeah." Kirk's area of expertise was canine rescue, not tracking, but over the years he'd worked side by side with skilled trackers and had picked up a fair amount of knowledge. "He's either heavy or travel-

ing with a big pack and moving fast. I'd estimate he
hiked up the mountain about four hours ago.''

Sara looked behind them as if expecting their pursuer to appear out of the woods. ''How long until we
reach the spot where the chopper can land?''

''A half hour?'' he guessed. ''That's if we don't
follow this man's tracks down the mountain.''

She pierced him with a frustrated look. ''Why
would we do that?''

''To see where he came from?''

Sara rolled her eyes at the sky. ''You want to take
Abby on a wild-goose chase up and down this mountain?''

''Of course not. But a man can't help his curiosity.'' He stood looking at the tracks, trying to glean
more information from the set of footprints. Although
he'd dearly love to confront the man who'd made
those tracks, his first obligation was to get Sara and
Abby to safety.

Sara tugged on his arm, her tone more insistent
than afraid. ''Come on, Kirk. Please. Let's get out of
here while we can.''

SARA WAITED with her sleeping baby while Kirk did
a perimeter sweep of the clearing. He'd been searching for a good hour to make sure that no one secretly
waited in ambush behind boulders or a heavy snowbank, and he had yet to return. Meanwhile, she
snacked on a power bar, thought about feeding Abby
soon and tried to control her impatience. Sara was
ready to be off this mountain. Ready for a hot shower,
a change of clothes and a cell phone signal.

She needed to call her contacts in California, let

them know she had the software so she could set up a new meeting. Only after completing the sale would she feel safe. Kirk had assured her that Logan Kincaid could arrange travel. Another twenty-four hours and the deal would be done.

She stomped her feet in the snow to help her circulation and glanced toward the direction in which Kirk had disappeared. She wished she'd asked him exactly how long he expected to be gone. She had no way of knowing if she should be concerned.

At least he'd left her the gun. The solid feel of the grip in her hand made her feel better. So did knowing that probably only one man was out there hunting them. After all, this mountain was huge.

Where was Kirk? She hadn't been around him for two full days and already the man occupied her thoughts much more than she would have liked. Of all the men she'd ever known, Kirk could be the most determined—and the most tender. Without her saying the words, he seemed to know so much—like how on edge she was about spending this time with him. He would have made the greatest of husbands...if he'd agreed to stay home. But the man had the heart of a gypsy. Even back in college, he'd used spring break to travel to the Florida Panhandle or to explore the coast of Maine. During his first hitch in the Marines, they'd explored whatever country they happened to be in. Now she knew better than to wait for him to end his roving ways.

Finally Kirk returned from checking out the clearing and signaled the chopper on the radio. Sara listened, holding her breath. She half expected the radio not to work. Or for no one to answer. But Logan Kincaid responded at Kirk's first hail.

"The chopper and Jack are on the way." Kincaid's voice came calmly through the radio. "Do you require medical assistance?"

"Not at this time," Kirk replied, clearly pleased that Jack was the man who would pick them up. He'd mentioned to her that during their flights to Colorado together, Kirk had come to respect both the man and his skill.

Kirk had already told her that he intended to keep the conversation short. Although she didn't understand how it was possible, she knew he worried that the other man whose tracks they'd seen on the mountain might triangulate their position from the brief radio conversation.

Kirk clicked off the radio. "Let's get out of sight."

He led her back from the clearing into the trees, where the thick pines would hide them from searchers. But she couldn't help feeling they were going in the wrong direction.

"But don't we want the chopper to be able to see us?" she asked.

"I sent them exact coordinates from my GPS. Jack Donovan knows where the clearing is to within twelve inches."

"And now so does that man whose tracks we saw."

"Exactly."

She read the worry in his eyes and tensed. Abby continued to sleep, although Sara imagined the baby would waken soon from hunger. "Do I have enough time to feed Abby before the rescue?"

He ordered Pepper to circle their location, and followed after the dog. "She'll give us warning if she spots anyone."

Sara woke the baby and fed her. Abby nursed quickly and had barely burped before she fell back to sleep in her sling. Sara had just finished buttoning her shirt and closing her jacket when the sound of the approaching helicopter had her looking skyward.

She wanted to run, waving her arms and shouting with happiness at the helicopter. Soon she would be warm, sitting in the heated aircraft on her way back to civilization.

Only the memory of Kirk's warning made her hold back, waiting impatiently for him to rejoin her. Sometimes Kirk could be overcautious. And she really didn't want to miss their ride.

Kirk and Pepper slipped out of the trees together. He came up next to her and took her hand, squeezing gently. "Ready?"

It would have been churlish to pull her hand from his. Besides, these might be their last moments alone together, and she did owe him. So she kept her hand in his, reminding herself not to get used to leaning on his strength.

She expected the helicopter to land in the middle of the clearing, but the vehicle circled the site's perimeter. Kirk already had his binoculars out and focused on the chopper.

He frowned. Must not have liked what he'd seen.

"That's not Jack piloting. Get back!"

Suddenly he yanked her against him and up against the tree, jamming their bodies among the branches.

Seconds later, bullets struck the snow where they'd just stood.

The man in the chopper was shooting at them.

"Abort. Abort." The words squawked from the radio, lending a warning much too late.

Kirk grabbed her hand again, yanking them away from the tree. "Run!"

Heart ramming against her ribs, she twisted Abby's carrier around to her chest and ran as fast as she could, slipping and sliding in the snow. With her free hand, she supported the back of Abby's neck, praying the jarring motion wouldn't hurt her, praying she wouldn't slip and fall on the baby.

Slowing down wasn't an option. They'd be shot.

At the sound of the chopper circling back, Kirk again found them cover against a tree. His arms closed around her, and his broad chest protected both her and the baby from the scratchy branches. Pepper huddled close to their legs.

"Abby's okay," he reassured her.

She looked down, amazed to see that her daughter had slept through all the commotion, except that the baby had been exhausted.

"Will they see our tracks?" she asked him, not bothering to keep her voice down. With the noise from the chopper, she didn't fear she'd be heard.

"Tracks are harder to see from the air, especially in this gray light. I'm hoping they may not have seen which way we ran, and expect us to run down the mountain."

Not up. The way he'd steered her to run. No wonder her lungs burned with the effort and her thigh muscles felt as though they'd been worked out on stair-climber equipment. A light sweat coated her skin, but underneath she was cold.

She tensed as the chopper passed directly overhead, the rotors blowing snow into their faces. Kirk shielded them as best he could, shouting into her ear. "Take deep breaths. Be prepared to run as soon as they head down the mountain."

She did as he instructed. But they couldn't keep going back up or they'd freeze to death before they got off the mountain. She didn't care how skilled Kirk was at this survival thing, they had to find a way down. Soon.

But first they had to avoid being shot. When Kirk deemed the chopper had turned far enough down the mountain, they trudged back up. The going slow. Every step an effort. Running in the steep snow was simply beyond her capability.

Kirk half carried, half dragged her back into the forest. He kept the pace brisk for half an hour until she demanded that they stop. Panting, she simply slid to the snow, too tired to speak, too tired to move.

"You did fine," he told her. "Rest."

He handed her the canteen and she drank, surprised by her thirst. It took several long minutes to regain her breath, but her sapped energy didn't return as easily.

"So did Logan turn on us?" she asked when she could again speak.

"He warned us at the last second over the radio. I believe the man is on our side. And that pilot wasn't Jack Donovan, although that was his chopper."

"So what do we do now? Contact Logan?"

"We could..."

Sara didn't like the way Kirk hadn't finished his sentence. While he might be perfectly comfortable tromping around on the snow-covered mountain being chased by who knew whom, she wanted to take her baby somewhere safe and warm. She wanted to sell her software, get rid of it and resume a normal, predictable life.

Without her saying a word, he seemed to know what she was thinking.

"Let's not make a hasty decision."

"What would you do if you were alone?" she asked.

"Find the man who's hunting us and demand some answers. Then, depending on those answers, I'd probably walk down to base camp."

Sara didn't like the hard, almost feral, expression in Kirk's eyes. She'd always known what he'd done for a living, but she'd never seen this side of him. In danger mode, his eyes gleamed with a fierce protectiveness that should have warned anyone intent on hurting them to back down.

"How far is Logan's camp?" she asked, summoning a courage she didn't know she had.

"Too far to start down today. You need a good night's sleep and food."

And he didn't?

Sara shook her head, suddenly too weary to argue. She didn't want to sleep in a cave or a snow hut or on the ground. She wanted a soft mattress, clean sheets and room service.

And she most certainly didn't want to spend another night alone with her ex-husband, cooped up beside a fire that he'd provided, eating food he'd supplied. She didn't want to owe him. Already he'd saved her from hunger and the cold, not to mention flying bullets.

And it appeared she had no choice but to spend another night in his care.

Chapter Eight

Kirk had asked her to go up the mountain for another hour before they traversed sideways over rocky terrain. He'd seemed pleased that they could walk for a long time without leaving tracks in the snow. Sara had just been glad not to have to pick her feet up so high with every step.

But in the open rocky spaces, the wind had ripped into her, eating up more energy reserves as her body fought to stay warm. Kirk had finally taken Abby inside his coat jacket to protect the baby from the chilling wind.

Finally they'd headed back down the mountain, but this time in a new direction. Sara concentrated on staying upright, and, when Kirk finally called a rest, she slumped into the snow exhausted. He handed her the baby, and she barely had the strength to hold and feed Abby.

Kirk built them a shelter out of his tarp, a snowbank and two pines, similar to her original snow hut, only slightly larger. He gathered firewood and started a fire, while she took care of a now-very-awake baby.

Abby, refreshed from sleeping all day, wanted to

get down and explore, crawl and play inside the shelter. Sara set her down next to Pepper. As Sara had hoped, Pepper kept Abby away from the flames just as protectively as she'd kept her own pups away from a fireplace in a house Sara and Kirk had once rented.

Kirk was making camp, and Sara knew she should help, but even the thought of shoving back to her feet required too much effort. As if sensing she'd come to the end of her stamina, Kirk crawled into the snow hut and sat beside her.

"How about some pine needle tea?"

He'd gathered handfuls of pine needles, and after melting snow in his pot, he tossed in the needles. A pleasant aroma filled the space. The heat combined with the pleasant scent must have made her nod off.

When she awakened, her head rested in Kirk's lap. Abby was playing with Pepper, safely away from the fire, and Kirk was holding hot food to her mouth. Without thinking, she parted her lips to eat, suddenly ravenous.

With hunger pangs came the awareness that she shouldn't have been sleeping at all, never mind with her head resting on Kirk's muscular thigh. She sat up slowly, still slightly groggy.

"How long did I sleep?"

"A few hours."

She glanced at the darkened walls and realized the sun had set hours ago.

"I don't think I've ever been that tired in my life."

"I figured you needed rest more than food, but now it's time to eat."

"Thanks." She took the fork and the hot meal, grateful for the few hours of uninterrupted sleep. As tired as she'd been, she'd never have been able to sleep if she hadn't known that he'd care for Abby.

Cheeks flushed and healthy-looking, Abby stood next to Pepper, holding onto the dog's neck, her balance unsteady. "Dog. Dog. Dog."

"Good girl," Kirk told her with a proud smile. He must have noticed Sara's raised eyebrows. "She's having a fine time and no worse for wear, except—"

"Except what?"

"We're going to run out of diapers tomorrow."

"That's a problem." Sara ate her food, pleased to see that Kirk was also eating. When he handed her the cup, she tasted his tea, surprised at the pleasant flavor. "It's good."

"We need to keep her dry to keep her warm. We'll have to hike out tomorrow." Kirk frowned at her. "If you're up to it."

"Do I have a choice?" she muttered, dropping her eyes to her food, uncomfortable with the way his gaze assessed her—with pity and pride. And desire.

She'd been married to the man way too long not to recognize the heat in his eyes. Although, the fact he could find her desirable when she'd been wearing the same clothes for three days and hadn't once brushed her hair or teeth said more for the strength of the male sex drive than it did about any attractiveness on her part.

"You surprised me today." He spoke softly, letting his fingers caress hers as he took back the cup and sipped his pine needle tea.

"Why?"

"Because athletes are accustomed to pushing their

bodies beyond their normal limits, but you aren't. Yet you held up well.''

''Every muscle in my body aches.''

His eyes glinted with amusement and banked heat. ''Want me to rub them for you?''

The image of his clever hands kneading her muscles almost elicited a groan, but she swallowed back the admission that she found his offer tempting.

''What I want is a hot bath, a cake of soap…and TV.''

He chuckled. ''And here I thought you were holding up so well that you didn't even miss civilization.''

She looked at him sitting cross-legged in front of the fire, the start of a beard shadowing his face. He looked as comfortable as he would have on their living room sofa, not the least aggravated by the cold or the lack of amenities.

''If we weren't in danger, I'd think you were enjoying yourself.''

''And if we weren't in danger, you'd be right.'' He paused. ''Otherwise, you wouldn't even be talking to me right now.''

''Don't go there,'' she warned him. She might be feeling more human after her nap, but she didn't have the strength for soul searching. She didn't want to have to battle her own inclinations as well as him, too. ''Tomorrow, are we going to just walk right into camp?''

''And hitch a ride back to Denver on the chopper? Yes.'' He answered the question for her, but she sensed he would walk in on his own terms and make his own demands.

While his take-charge attitude might once have

bothered her, she felt safe letting him make the decisions until they were back in civilization. Tomorrow wouldn't be easy. She expected to say goodbye to him, again. And she didn't feel good about her decision to keep father and daughter apart. In fact, she felt damn guilty.

AFTER THEY BOTH FINISHED EATING, Kirk built up the fire with enough heavy wood to burn through the cold hours of the night. The baby, all tuckered out from her busy day, had fallen asleep next to her new best friend, Pepper. And guided by maternal instinct, the dog curled her body protectively around the child as if guarding her from any possibility of accidentally rolling into the fire.

Kirk sensed a certain softening in Sara's attitude toward him—not so much from her words, but she seemed less reserved, less on guard. When she scooted onto her back, her hip touching his in the small space, he pillowed his arm under her head.

Eyes wide, she turned her head to look at him, the firelight reflecting confusion on her face. "This isn't a good idea."

"What?"

"Our sleeping so close."

She'd spoken gently and didn't pull away, obviously conflicted about her feelings. On their first night on the mountain, she'd edged away, determined to not so much as brush against him. Now, she seemed not to know what she wanted, and he took her confusion as a sign that he was making progress.

He didn't make any comment about sharing body

heat. Sara didn't play those kinds of games. She made up her mind and stuck to her guns.

If he'd had more time, he wouldn't have pushed his luck. But tomorrow they would return to civilization, and he might never have this opportunity again.

Kirk placed his hand on her shoulder and drew her more firmly against his side.

She sighed. "You never were any good at listening."

"Not when listening goes against what I want."

"And what do you want, Kirk?"

"You."

"Yeah, sure." Her voice tightened. "For how long will you want me?"

"Forever," he admitted, hoping he wouldn't scare her away by his admission of the truth.

"But that won't be enough to keep you at home when the next mission comes your way. And they always ask for you—because you're so good at what you do. If you hadn't found us, Abby and I wouldn't even be alive right now. So I know I owe you, but that doesn't mean I want to spend the rest of my life paying you back."

"Don't," he chided.

"Don't what?"

"Pretend that you're letting me hold you out of gratitude. I know better."

"Do you know that you broke my heart?" She could tell her words wounded him as she had meant for them to do, but he didn't release her. "Do you know I cried myself to sleep every night for a month after our divorce went through? Do you know that you've damaged me?''

''I'm so sorry,'' he whispered, damning himself for hurting her so badly, hating the way he could still hear the pain in her voice. He wanted to kiss away her hurt, not knowing if that was possible, not quite daring to try.

''I can't even look at other men. The manager at the grocery store asked me out. He has a nice, safe job. Comes homes every day. He's intelligent and healthy, and all I could think was that he wasn't you. And if you say *good,* I'm going to slap you,'' she warned.

''Good.'' He grinned and lazily waited for her raised hand, took enjoyment in capturing her wrist and drawing her onto his chest.

''You don't have to look so satisfied,'' she muttered, scowling. ''I'm still angry with you.''

''I know.''

Her eyes narrowed in speculation and then she sighed. ''There's really only one good way to shut you up.''

He held his breath.

She dipped her head and kissed him, not the least bit hesitantly. Her mouth crushed against his, claiming him, branding him, and he reciprocated eagerly. Sara didn't bother with fancy technique; she thrust her tongue into his mouth, demanding, taking, searching.

He'd forgotten how she could go from zero to sixty in less than a heartbeat. He'd forgotten how she put her entire body into a kiss. As usual, once she made up her mind, she didn't hold back. She went top speed, so that a man could barely keep up with her shifts in desire.

But his body remembered, responding immediately to her familiar scent and taste. His pulse rate ignited, his blood burning with powerful needs that hadn't been satisfied in too long. All the blood in his body went south, until his arousal pressed tightly into the seam of his jeans.

His need was as strong as the wind blowing outside and just as elemental. So when she pulled back, breathless, her cheeks flushed, her eyes glazed with desire and a hint of regret, he had to muster every ounce of control not to draw her back down again.

"I just wanted you to know how much I missed you," she explained. "Our kiss changes nothing."

"Some men would call you a tease."

"But you know me better than that. If I could have held you with my body and sex, we wouldn't have gotten divorced."

She might as well have kicked him in the balls. That she could make the admission so bravely, facing her fears and presumed inadequacies so squarely, made him curse. "You act as though I wanted to leave you."

But he had had a choice and he'd made the wrong one. He could have quit the work that had taken him away from her, that had left her with too many lonely hours contemplating the danger he walked into every day. To give her credit, she didn't say a word. She just shot him that you-know-better look and rolled onto her side, her back to him.

Conversation over.

Marriage over.

Damn. Damn. Damn.

He ached to reach out to her, smooth her hair from her forehead and reassure her that he'd changed. He knew now that he should have put Sara first. He no longer felt as though he alone had to stop the next terrorist attack. With maturity earned the hard way, he had come to the realization that others *could* fill his shoes, maybe not as well, but they would learn as he had. Kirk had given enough, had served his country honorably and well, and now he was entitled to enjoy some peace.

Sara's leaving had created a gaping hole inside him that a new mission couldn't fill.

And when he realized what he'd lost, he'd turned to her too late. He'd hurt her so badly that she was afraid to give him the trust she'd once offered.

Kirk stared into the fire, his mind seething with could-haves, should-haves and would-haves. He couldn't go back and undo the past. He could only go forward and vow not to repeat his mistakes.

Beside him, Sara's breath rose and fell evenly, but from her tensed shoulders, he could tell that she hadn't fallen asleep. Lost in her own thoughts, she'd shut him out yet again.

The wind outside still howled, but he heard nothing alarming. Pepper suddenly raised her head, her ears high. The animal's hearing was sixty times more acute than a man's. Did she hear a wild animal? The chopper returning?

Or had the other man on the mountain followed his nose to their campfire?

SARA HEARD KIRK SCOOT through the snow hut's entrance and figured he needed to answer a call of nature. Softly, he ordered Pepper to stay, before disappearing into the night.

The dog whined, obeying the command but clearly not happy at being left behind. The moment Kirk vanished, Sara expected Pepper to rest her chin back down on her paws. But she kept her head and ears up, staring anxiously after Kirk.

Sara sat up and scratched Pepper behind the ears. "What is it, girl?"

She'd been around Kirk and his animals long enough to know that the dogs had acute senses well beyond the range of human beings. They also displayed fearless loyalty, often risking their own lives to save their two-legged counterparts.

Pepper didn't stand, but her gaze went from Sara back to where Kirk had departed. The few other times he'd left the animal behind, Pepper hadn't appeared this concerned. Her big brown eyes seemed to be begging Sara to follow Kirk out into the darkness.

At the sound of flesh striking flesh, Sara's heart kicked into overdrive. Someone was out there.

Someone had found them.

From the thuds and grunts, she guessed that Kirk was fighting. For their lives. Adrenaline kicked in and her thoughts raced at megawatt speed.

Crawling to Kirk's pack, Sara clawed down into the recesses until her hands closed over the gun. She checked the clip and slipped off the safety, her heart battering her ribs in panic. She trusted Kirk's ability to protect them, but he could have been jumped in the dark, outnumbered or taken by surprise. He could be injured.

But surely he would have shouted if he wanted her help. Maybe he'd taken a blow to the throat and couldn't yell? Or perhaps he didn't want her to walk into danger. It would be just like the stubborn man to bravely lie there bleeding to death in the snow, refusing to put her in jeopardy.

If she'd thought she could save their daughter by letting Kirk sacrifice himself, she might do so. But staying hidden in the snow hut, hoping their pursuer wouldn't find her, wasn't an option. The scent of their campfire could be smelled for miles—had probably led the man right to their front door.

She had to hurry. Decide what to do.

Kirk could even now be lying outside, unconscious.

Sara glanced at her sleeping child. *Oh God.* Should she leave her? While Pepper wouldn't allow the baby to crawl too close to the fire, if Sara and Kirk didn't return, the baby wouldn't survive. No one would find her. No one would even know where to look.

But without Kirk, neither Sara nor Abby might survive the hour. And perhaps with Kirk fighting and distracting his opponent, she could alter the outcome in their favor.

The sound of a guttural curse made up her mind for her.

After one last look at her sleeping baby, Sara crawled out the entrance. It took several moments for her eyes to adjust to the darkness outside. In those seconds the icy wind chilled her from her nose to her toes. Her body immediately began to shiver and shake, although the trembling might have been her reaction to spiking fear.

Sara pulled the gun up inside her sleeve to protect

her hand from the bitter cold. If her fingers went numb from the icy metal gun, she wouldn't be able to pull the trigger. Perhaps she should have worn gloves, but she didn't feel comfortable handling the weapon through bulky material.

Where was Kirk?

When she'd been inside the snow hut, they'd sounded close by, but now she saw no sign of men fighting. Just the black, black sky concealing the towering trees amid the gray-black snow. With the wind howling at her, she couldn't hear anything beyond the frantic roar of fear in her ears.

Turning her back to the wind gained her a respite from the bitter cold and allowed her to recognize several man-size grunts. Hefting the gun, she plodded through deep snow, uphill, in the direction from which the sounds had come. While the adrenaline urged her to run, she'd do Kirk no good if she rushed in blindly and got taken as a hostage.

There.

She saw a flash of movement. Dark silhouettes rolling across the ground.

Two men, their hands clasping one another's throats in death grips, the bodies rolling and tumbling so she couldn't tell Kirk from his foe.

Of similar height and weight, the men seemed evenly matched, first one of them gaining the advantage and rolling on top, then the other. She kept her distance, waiting for the right moment, fearful of making a mistake and shooting the wrong man.

She thought of calling out, asking Kirk to identify himself, but she didn't dare distract him. The men used knee strikes to the gut, and rammed elbows into one another's faces and necks, tumbling down the mountain and knocking into trees, boulders and snow-banks.

Sara followed, coming a little closer, careful not to get caught in their fray. For a moment, she thought she recognized Kirk, but then the men rolled again and she lost track of who was who.

Frustrated, she considered shooting straight up and ordering them to stop fighting. But suppose they didn't listen?

She had the gun. She ought to be able to *do* something. But what?

Striking someone on the head could be a bad move, since she couldn't tell Kirk from his attacker. Frustrated that she could think of nothing to help, she edged closer.

The men tumbled, punched and kicked, their thick clothing protecting them from all but the heaviest blows. Their breathing labored, yet strong, the men fought in eerie silence, both of them apparently still unaware of her presence.

She had to end this fight. Separate them somehow.

Pepper would have known immediately which man was which. Even if blinded, the dog could have picked out Kirk by smell. While Sara couldn't depend on scent, she knew his body as well as she knew her own. She'd been married to the man for over seven years. And she knew the graceful way he moved, never jerky, always in balance—which didn't help, since both men seemed to have the same skilled movements.

The rolling men separated and, breathing heavily, slowly got to their feet. Facing one another, neither appeared to notice her. One of the men cursed loud, long and hard, and she knew that man was not Kirk Hardaker.

She fired a shot into the air. And aimed the weapon at the stranger. ''Don't move or the next bullet—''

The man lunged and dived down the mountain, somersaulting at a cockeyed angle. She hesitated. She'd fired a weapon before, but firing at a moving, living person was entirely different from shooting at a lifeless target.

Still, that man could come back to kill her baby. Just as she squeezed the trigger, Kirk held up his hand. She heard him speak over the gun's retort.

''Wait! Don't shoot him.''

He'd spoken a second too late. She'd already fired.

The man she'd shot stopped rolling, and nausea churned in her stomach. She'd killed him, taken a life, and she thought she might be sick.

Kirk came up beside her and took the gun from her trembling fingers. ''You okay?''

''No. Is he…''

''Stay here and I'll check.''

Her knees shook so badly that she slid onto her butt in the snow, drew her knees in to her chest and rested her cheeks on her knees. She didn't want to look, didn't want to face what she had done.

''He's dead, but you didn't kill him.''

''What?'' She lifted her head and stared at Kirk, who had rolled the body to its back. Sara was glad of the dark that prevented her from looking at the man's face.

''You missed.''

Kirk sounded so sure, and relief pumped through her. "Then, what killed him?"

"He broke his neck."

He'd died, but not by her hand. A smidgen of warmth flowed back into her frozen flesh. She ceased rocking and shoved her hands into her pockets to warm her cold fingers.

Kirk searched the body, no doubt checking for a wallet, but he found nothing to identify the man. "He's a professional. There's nothing on him to lead us to his boss—if he has one. But men like him don't give the orders."

"How do you know?" Her gunshot might not have killed him directly, but if she hadn't interfered, the man might still be alive for Kirk to ask his questions.

"I'm just guessing, but the attempts to steal your work have been systematic and too thorough to be the work of just one man. Your house was burglarized, then the plane accident arranged. I'm assuming this man is not the pilot of your plane?" Kirk removed the man's hat.

She didn't want to look, but shoved to her feet and forced herself to evaluate his features. The pilot had had swarthy skin and dark hair. This man was lightly tanned and had blond hair. "You're right. They aren't the same. Which means there isn't just one person after me."

Kirk placed a comforting arm over her shoulder. "Let's just hope that now we're alone on this mountain."

Chapter Nine

Sara and Kirk returned to the snow hut, where Pepper greeted Kirk with an enthusiastic *woof* and the swipe of her friendly tongue along the back of his hand. Abby still slept, looking relaxed and at peace. He wished he could say the same for Sara.

The violence had drawn her deep into herself. After her initial assessment that his attacker was not her pilot, she hadn't said a word. Not even after they'd crawled into their shelter.

He melted snow in their pot and used the last of their instant coffee to make a steaming drink, then handed her the cup. "Drink this."

"Thanks." She took several sips, then passed him the cup to share. Staring into the fire, she seemed lost in her thoughts. The fight and the man's death had obviously upset her, but he knew she didn't blame him for this incident. Sara was always fair. She'd known he'd been attacked and had had no choice. But he didn't like reminding her of what he'd once been, didn't want her thinking that he couldn't change what he was.

She stirred the fire with a stick. "That man fought like you did."

"What do you mean?" He gazed into her eyes, thinking her observation odd but glad that she was willing to talk to him. Instead of shutting him out and making him prod her thoughts from her, she was sharing, voluntarily.

"He used the same movements you used. Almost as if he'd had the same training."

Kirk thought back to the fight, assessing the punches and counter-punches. He'd immediately recognized his opponent's skills in hand-to-hand combat, but in the heat of battle he hadn't analyzed the man's attack. He hadn't used martial arts. Nor had he fought like a street fighter. "You think he was military?"

"Maybe he learned to fight in the same place you did. When I was trying to figure out which man was you, I watched the telltale movements."

"You did good not to shoot first. Thanks."

"You have this smooth way of walking and punching. He had that, too."

Sara might not know the difference between a jab and an uppercut, but she'd noticed details infinitely more interesting.

"Are any of your competitors ex-marines?" he asked.

She shrugged and reached for the coffee. "I have no idea. If I had Internet access, I could check."

He raised his brow. "By hacking into the government's database?"

"Or their bank accounts, to see if they receive a military pension." She grinned at him, her eyes fiery with the challenge. "And, no, I haven't been hacking.

Not since you lectured me back in college about how you couldn't sleep at night due to worry that I would be arrested.''

He'd asked her to stop and she had. Not that she ever did anything to harm the Web sites. She'd simply enjoyed the challenge of getting inside. When he'd explained that her shenanigans could ruin his reputation and his career, she'd immediately stopped her activities. But he had no doubt she still had the skills to do a little illegal checking around.

"We should have an Internet connection by tonight."

Her eyes widened at his implication that this time he wouldn't condemn her hacking the information they needed. But she didn't gloat. Sara never gloated or boasted over her amazing computer skills.

"So we're going down the mountain in the morning?"

He nodded. "We've only seen the one set of tracks during our time here, and those footprints probably belonged to the dead man. Hopefully he was working alone, and we'll have no problems on the way down. But just in case—"

"Yeah?"

"I'd like to take Pepper out for a little nighttime recon. Will you be okay, if I leave you with the gun?"

"Do I have a choice?"

"If you want me to stay, I'll stay. I'd just like to have an idea of what we might be facing tomorrow."

She made up her mind. "How long will you be gone?"

"Just an hour or so. I'll call out the code word *salt*

before I crawl back in, so you don't shoot me by accident.''

Kirk did a perimeter check, circling the camp, as well as following their foe's tracks down the mountain. He found evidence of a campfire, but no second set of tracks. Much relieved, he returned to Sara and Abby, determined to get a few hours of sleep before they set out in the morning.

But when he called out the prearranged code word *salt,* Sara didn't answer.

WITH THE GUN IN HER HAND, Sara had fallen asleep. Relief swept through Kirk as he listened to her regular breathing. Gently he lifted the weapon from her grasp and lay down beside her. The toll of the past few days had clearly sapped Sara's strength, or she'd never have fallen asleep while on watch. Although she hadn't complained, Kirk realized he'd pushed her beyond her limits.

One more day, he promised silently. And then he would take her someplace safe where she could rest and recuperate. He fed the fire to allow them to sleep a few extra hours in the morning, then shut his eyes. Within minutes he too was asleep.

The next morning Kirk awakened to Sara breast-feeding the baby. She held Abby close to her chest, the baby's head nestled in the crook of her arm. Abby made contented sucking noises, smacking her lips and gulping noisily.

Sara noted Kirk's interest and smiled at him. ''I don't think I'll ever get used to the miracle of her birth. Holding her, feeding her, is a constant reminder that she belongs to me.''

"To us." His words slipped out before he'd thought about the wisdom of challenging her statement. "We created her together. She's *our* daughter."

He didn't think he'd ever seen a sight so moving as Sara feeding their child. The baby kept her fingers splayed on Sara's breast, which was rounded and filled with milk. And when the baby released the erect pink nipple, he couldn't help wishing for a taste.

However he dared not move in her direction, content that Sara was willing to share this special moment. "What does feeding her feel like?"

"Strange, tingly, good. It's difficult to explain."

Kirk refrained from licking his lips. "Does she bite?"

Sara shook her head, rearranged her bra, then shifted the baby to her other breast. Apparently accustomed to the routine, Abby latched on immediately and continued to suck contentedly.

Sara's eyes glowed with pride and a hint of amusement. "I wish I had a camera to capture the look of wonder on your face."

"I'm the one who needs a camera. The two of you are beautiful."

Sara didn't blush. She appeared so natural and at ease with her body and the baby that he marveled at the change in her. He thought of Sara as brilliant and sexy, now he had to add maternal.

She brushed the hair from her eyes. "I'm sorry I fell asleep while you were gone last night."

"It's okay. I've pushed you pretty hard. Today should be the last difficult day, and then you can rest." He sat up and fed the fire. "I didn't find any more tracks, but I still want to be careful."

"What do you mean?"

"I'd like to sneak into Logan Kincaid's camp, kidnap his pilot and force him to fly us to Denver."

"I thought you trusted the man."

"I do. But someone could be watching his camp, waiting for him to help us."

He knew she understood, because she changed the subject. "We need diapers. I'm going to use one after Abby's done eating. Then we'll only have one left."

"Logan has baby stuff stored in a tent. We'll stop there before heisting the chopper."

"Okay." She hesitated. "You know, I appreciate everything you've done for us."

"Don't."

"Don't what?"

"I hear a *but* hanging in the air, and I really don't want to hear you say more. Not today." Not ever.

"There's something you need to hear," she insisted. "I didn't want to share Abby—especially after you never answered my letters. But now that I know you didn't get them, and now that I've had time to think, I've changed my mind. Keeping you two apart is not fair to her, or to you. So we'll work out visitation."

Despite her calmly worded statements, he knew the offer hadn't been easy for her to make. And he appreciated that she had softened her stance, but he wanted more. He didn't require her permission to share Abby. But he hadn't been married to Sara for years without learning when to keep his mouth shut.

Sometimes a good marriage was based not so much on what one said but what one didn't say. He kept in mind the important concession she'd made and the others he was determined to win from her. But he didn't want just visiting rights, he wanted to help Sara raise Abby.

They ate the last of their food, drank pine needle tea since the coffee was gone, and set out at about ten o'clock. While the sun had yet to show from behind the clouds, the bitter cold from the night had dissipated and the snow had stopped falling.

Kirk broke trail, but he was careful to allow ample rest stops. During one rest, he and Pepper circled their perimeter but came across no additional tracks. Kirk didn't believe anyone else was tailing them.

Last night during his recon, he'd buried the dead man beneath rocks to keep the animals away and had carefully marked the spot. He intended to ask Logan's men to return for the body, and he hoped fingerprints or dental work might lead them to a positive identification, and eventually to whoever had sent the man after Sara and Kirk.

They'd been walking for two hours when Sara stopped and rubbed her shoulder. "How much farther?"

He reached into his pocket, took out his GPS and read the dial. "About a half hour. Why?"

"Abby needs a diaper change. She tends to cry when she's wet for too long. And you said that you wanted to sneak into the camp which—"

"—will be impossible with a crying baby." He finished her sentence for her and reevaluated his plan. "How would you feel about waiting here with Abby while I steal some supplies?"

"Can you leave me the gun, or will you need it?"

He looked at Sara and realized once again that she

had a very intelligent mind. On the surface her question seemed innocent and clear, but she really wanted to know if he felt he was walking into danger. His taking the gun would be a clear admission of danger. Since the subject of his putting his life in jeopardy was a sore spot between them, she hadn't asked her question outright.

He owed her a truthful response, but he had no idea what he might face when he returned to Logan's camp. His use of stealth might be totally unnecessary, but he preferred to remain cautious, with Sara's and Abby's lives at stake.

"You can keep the weapon and my pack. I'll travel faster light."

"And what should I do if you don't come back?"

She'd asked the question calmly, but he could hear the underlying fear in her tone. And if her voice hadn't told him of her concern for his safety, the way she bravely lifted her chin and squared her shoulders would have. He could tell her there was no cause for worry, but he wouldn't lie to her.

"I have every intention of coming back—but if I can't, go to Logan Kincaid."

"We haven't heard from him since the aborted helicopter pickup."

"Exactly. He's waiting for us to come out, and giving us every opportunity to do it by ourselves— which is the safest way possible."

"I'm not sure I follow…"

"If he used the radio to call us, others could listen in and locate us. If he sent up the chopper to search, he could clue in anyone watching him to our location and put us in more danger."

"You're saying that he's helping us—"

"By letting *me* get you out." Kirk liked the confidence Logan displayed by patiently waiting for him to bring Abby and Sara to safety. Logan had earned his respect—if not his complete trust—but that end of the operation could have been compromised through no fault of the Shey Group. "So even if I accidentally bump into Logan's men, I won't need a gun."

"You're willing to risk your life, but not ours?"

"I'm just being careful. If Logan wanted you, he wouldn't have brought me into the mix. But someone could be watching Logan's camp, expecting me to bring you in."

"So you're just being careful?"

"Yes. And Abby needs those diapers. If we have to steal the chopper, I'd like her quiet. Is there anything else you need?"

She shook her head. "Just come back, soon."

KIRK HAD LEFT PEPPER with Sara and Abby. The dog played with the baby on the blanket Sara had floated over the snow. Sara marveled at Abby's ability to adapt. Her daughter didn't seem to mind the cold, the lack of her usual toys or her new wintry surroundings. As long as her daughter had Pepper and Sara, she was happy, reminding Sara of Abby's oh-so-adaptable father. Kirk thrived in survival mode, thinking on his feet and adjusting to the situation with instincts that often saved lives.

Although concern over Kirk sneaking into and out of Logan's camp niggled, Sara forced herself to rest. A body and mind could take only so much stress before adjusting to danger. Sara sprawled on the blanket and enjoyed Abby's repeated attempts to pull herself to her feet and take a few steps before falling on her bottom. Laughing. And making the attempt all over again.

"Dog. Dog. Dog!" Abby squealed.

Sara gazed at her daughter fondly, but after Pepper stood and growled low in her throat, her hackles rising, Sara swept Abby into her arms. The dog hadn't snarled at the baby; she was looking at the mountain. What had alarmed Pepper?

"Dog. Dog." Abby clapped her hands together with glee, then pointed.

It wasn't dogs, but wolves—three of them—stalking toward them, and Sara's blood chilled. Holding Abby tightly, Sara lunged for Kirk's pack and the gun he had left behind.

She dug awkwardly with one hand past the first aid kit and radio. Finally her fingers closed around the weapon. She yanked the gun out, but in her haste and fear, she dropped it in the snow.

The wolves were closing in. She had to pick up the gun.

Bending clumsily as she held Abby, Sara retrieved the snow-covered weapon while keeping her eyes on the approaching wolves.

These animals, wild and scrawny enough for their ribs to stick out, fanned into attack position, hostile and hungry. A multitude of growls challenged and taunted Pepper. The German shepherd responded by placing herself protectively between the wolves and Sara and Abby. Pepper's attitude couldn't have been more clear. To get to Sara and the baby, the wolves would have to go through her.

Pepper, larger and healthier than the wolves, was nonetheless outnumbered three to one. She faced the wild wolves, barking and growling sharp warnings.

At Pepper's noise, the wolves hesitated. Sara fumbled with the gun, then pulled the trigger.

The gun jammed.

As if sensing weakness, the wolves attacked Pepper, snapping, biting, circling. The dog gave as good as she got.

Hearing the ferocious fighting, Abby realized something was wrong and started to scream. At the sound of her cries, the wolves backed off, licked the insignificant wounds Pepper had inflicted and seemed to reconsider their strategy. But their eyes never once glanced away from their prey.

Sara didn't want to take her gaze off the wolves, either, fearing they might take her looking away as a sign of cowardice, encouragement to attack. But she had to clear the snow from the gun—not an easy thing to do while holding the baby. However, no way would she put Abby down within reach of those vicious teeth.

Mittens hampered her movements and she wasted precious seconds to pull them off. In that moment, the wolves decided that Abby's noise wasn't a factor. And attacked again. They charged as a unit.

Valiantly, Pepper fought, her jaws snapping and chewing, her legs jumping and twisting in movements so fast that she blurred. And again the wolves retreated, panting and bloody, but by no means giving up. Pepper licked at a trickle of blood running down her leg, but she didn't lower her guard, remaining between her people and the pack.

Sara frantically brushed the snow from the gun and blew air into the chamber, hoping to clear the excess moisture and ice.

"Come on. Come on. Come on." She aimed the gun in the direction of the wolves. And fired.

Abby screamed at the loud *bang*. Sara squeezed the trigger again.

At the gunshots, the wolves retreated, melting into the trees. But Sara could not be sure they wouldn't be back. She needed to build a fire. But she couldn't carry wood and Abby, too. And no way was she putting the screaming baby down.

Sara was trembling so hard she could barely hold the gun and feared she might drop Abby. She slipped on the gun's safety and called Pepper back to the blanket. The dog licked the baby's tears, and Abby went from crying to smiling in less than five seconds.

Sara wished she could so easily put the scary incident behind her. She rocked Abby in her lap, petted Pepper. "Good dog."

Sara knew she should tend to the dog's injury. Kirk had left a first aid kit in his pack. But she couldn't stop trembling and the dog's injury didn't look serious. Pepper set about cleaning her wound with her tongue while Abby watched in fascination.

Sara's trembling wouldn't stop. Those wolves could have killed them. If Pepper hadn't protected them, if the gun hadn't finally worked, they might be wolf dinner right about now. And it would have been her fault. For not keeping better watch, for relaxing and letting down her guard, for dropping the gun in the snow.

She didn't belong in the woods. She hated her inability to control this wild environment—much preferred her office where she controlled every keystroke, where surprises weren't deadly, where logic ruled. Out here, she never knew what to expect next, and the strain made her feel damn incompetent.

She hugged Abby, grateful she was okay, and uncontrollable tears of relief streamed from Sara's eyes and down her cheeks. Angry at her inability to restrain her slowly subsiding panic, she sniffled, determined to get herself back under control. But the sobs inside her had a will of their own. As if summoned by the wolves' departure, grief racked her.

And that's how Kirk found her, sitting and crying and holding Abby, while Pepper snuggled next to them. Kirk hurried to them, his gaze taking in Pepper's injury, the tracks, the wolves' blood in the snow.

He settled next to her on the blanket, lifted Abby into the crook of his arm and held Sara close with the other. "I heard your gunshots. Are you all right?"

"I want to go home." Her words came out in a sob. "I don't belong out here in the woods. I almost got us killed. When the wolves attacked, I dropped the gun in the snow and it jammed. If Pepper hadn't... Is she okay?"

"Looks like a scratch. I'll clean and bandage her wound later. Right now, I'm more concerned about you and Abby. I brought diapers."

She brushed away the tears. "Any trouble?"

Kirk frowned. "It was too easy. Almost as if Logan knew I was coming and had cleared the route."

She hiccuped and leaned into Kirk, grateful for his warmth and strength and support. Not only did he help her keep the panic at bay, but he would never make fun of her weakness. He never berated her when she made the wrong decisions. He would never blame her for dropping the gun and almost getting them killed. In fact, he was gazing down at her with adoration and pride, looking just as handsome as he had wearing his dress uniform in their wedding pictures.

His eyes gleamed with kindness, and she swallowed back more tears. "Why are you looking at me like that? I fell apart. I'm no good out here."

He raised one skeptical eyebrow. "Oh, really? I don't know another woman who could start a fire with baby diapers and her computer."

"I had no choice."

"Or a woman who could build a snow hut in a blizzard."

"The Inuit have built igloos for the past ten thousand years. I wouldn't consider my little hut a major accomplishment."

"And you may have dropped the gun, but you didn't run stupidly in fear."

"I wanted to run."

"But you didn't—which would most certainly have gotten you hurt."

"I panicked."

"You got the gun working in time."

"Barely."

"You stayed and faced down the wolves."

"Then I fell apart."

"Not until after the crisis had passed. You didn't just do good. You did real, real good."

His words didn't comfort her much, not when she realized how close she and their daughter had come, once again, to dying. "I was so scared."

"You'd have to be an idiot not to be scared."

He placed the baby on his lap, dug into his pack, removed a tissue and held it to Sara's nose so she wouldn't have to remove her mittens again.

"Blow."

He wiped her nose as if she were Abby—not a grown woman. And she liked letting him take care of her. Liked knowing that he would protect Abby and that she could rely on him to ensure their safety. Sara had never imagined that caring for Abby would include fighting off wolves or surviving plane crashes or mountain storms.

Right now, Sara needed Kirk, but she didn't want to depend on him. She'd known that being a single mother would make enormous demands on her time and emotions. But while she hadn't expected loving her baby to be so rewarding, she hadn't been prepared for so many failures.

She'd almost gotten her baby killed—several times. That Kirk didn't blame her didn't change the facts. Raising her daughter had turned into a challenge she wasn't sure she'd had the right to take by herself. It was bad enough that she'd placed herself in danger, but she had no right to do that to her child.

And as much as she wanted to depend on Kirk, she'd already gone that route. He couldn't be the permanent solution to her problems. Not when she couldn't count on him to be there tomorrow. Although she was beginning to believe that he wouldn't re-up, the job offer with the Shey Group remained open. And the land of his ranch—merely leased. He could pack up and head for distant shores at any time.

But she had him now, and watched him gently draw Abby near, lay her across his lap and change her diaper with an expertise that amazed her. He'd always been good with his hands. And he seemed to know just when to distract the baby so he could snap first her jammies shut and then her snowsuit back together. He also seemed to know that, at the moment, Sara was incapable of doing much more than watch him take care of their child.

She had to get a grip.

Gather her strength.

But all she really wanted to do was stay at Kirk's side and let him take charge of their safety. Sara didn't want this life and death kind of responsibility, wasn't qualified to make these kinds of decisions. Being on this mountain wasn't anything like the computer war games she'd often played on the Internet. This was real. The results deadly.

Gradually Sara's sobs diminished. With her eyes red and puffy from crying, she must look like a wreck. But Abby, Kirk and Pepper didn't seem to mind or even notice. Taking off her mittens, she threaded her fingers through her hair, trying to neaten her appearance.

Kirk took out the first aid kit and tended to Pepper, who held surprisingly still while he applied antibiotic ointment. However, when he reached for the gauze to wrap her leg, she moved away a few steps. Clearly, she was familiar with gauze and didn't want her leg wrapped.

"Okay, girl," Kirk agreed. "You're going to be

fine,'' he told the dog in a reassuring voice meant to settle the injured animal.

Sara suspected he also said the words to encourage her.

Finally she pulled herself back together. Kirk waited until she'd calmed, then urged her onto her feet and back down the mountain, the way he'd come. As if sensing that just walking took all of her strength, he'd insisted on carrying Abby, who had gotten quite accustomed to her father. The baby smiled up at him, no longer the least bit shy or nervous around the huge man with the deep voice.

Abby clapped her hands together. "Good dog."

"Very good dog," he agreed. They looked back over his shoulder at Sara, who trailed behind. "I saw no one at the camp," Kirk told her again. "Hopefully, we can go straight to the chopper. You can wait there while I find the pilot and convince him to fly us out."

"Suppose the pilot won't cooperate?"

Kirk's voice turned grim. "I don't intend to give him a choice."

They walked down the mountain without any more surprises. When they neared Logan's camp, Kirk handed her the baby. He also removed the gun from his pack and placed the weapon in his jacket pocket. Kirk didn't hide his action from her, but he didn't comment, either.

They circled the camp's outskirts and saw no one. They heard voices from inside a large tent, as if Logan's entire team had gathered inside. Maybe to eat? Or for a briefing?

Beside her, Kirk spoke in a whisper. "I can't believe they haven't posted even one guard. Logan Kincaid is a lot of things, but he isn't sloppy.''

"Maybe he thinks we're dead," she suggested.

"Then, why is he still here?"

"You're the expert. You tell me."

"I can't. His operation is professional. All of his team—at least, those I've met or spoken with—seem top-notch. Yet he's left this place wide open to us. Almost as if he expects us."

Kirk in front, they circled close to the helicopter that sat in a clearing. They would have to leave the cover of the forest to approach, and her pulse raced.

Kirk motioned her to stay back among the trees. "Remain here while I check—"

"We go together," Sara insisted.

"There is no reason to put you in danger. Let me—"

"No." Sara recalled the attacking wolves and was determined not to be left behind. "If something happens to you, we won't stand a chance by ourselves. Right now, the safest place on this mountain is right behind you."

"Okay. Keep your voice down."

"Like there's anyone around to hear?" The camp's emptiness in broad daylight spooked her. So did the sight of the chopper sitting squarely in base camp— the same chopper that had fired on them back in the woods. How had the chopper gotten back here, and why did it appear as if it had never left?

The sound of men's voices coming from that tent didn't reassure her. Once they made it to the chopper, Kirk had to find the pilot. "Convince" him to fly them out. And Kirk wouldn't stand a chance against an armed group of men. He'd have to wait until he could get the pilot alone.

Sara swallowed back her fear. She and Abby and Pepper might have to wait for hours alone in the chopper while Kirk scoured the camp for Jack Donovan. But she could shut the door against four-legged predators, she told herself in an attempt to boost her spirits.

Kirk and Sara broke from the woods, Pepper at their side, and half walked, half loped to the chopper. No one from the tent seemed to notice. No guard called out. No dogs barked.

Kirk opened the chopper door. Climbed one step. And a dark-haired man aimed a gun at Kirk's temple.

Chapter Ten

"Welcome aboard." Jack Donovan waved Kirk, Sara, Abby and Pepper inside the helicopter with his gun. "I've been expecting you."

Sara looked at Kirk with huge question marks in her eyes, but he had to give her credit; she didn't panic. Didn't say a word, letting him handle this situation as he saw fit. Sara had this uncanny knack of setting her ego and brilliant mind aside and letting him take charge, once she'd decided they were in his area of expertise.

That Jack had been expecting him could mean several things. Good or bad. Perhaps Logan's team had been tracking Kirk from the beginning. The man had supplied Kirk's equipment and easily could have hidden a tracking device inside the first aid kit or even in the cash or the baby's sling. Or someone Kirk hadn't seen had been following them. Or perimeter guards had picked up their entrance into camp, but had let them through.

None of these possibilities was necessarily in and of itself ominous. But Kirk burned with curiosity over what exactly Logan was thinking. Friend or foe, the man was clever. Kirk hoped he was a friend, because he suspected the man could think circles around most military strategists.

When Jack repocketed his weapon, Kirk didn't automatically relax. He hadn't forgotten that another pilot had shown up in Jack's chopper at the clearing in the woods—and that pilot had shot at them. Kirk needed an explanation for that fiasco, but knew that if the explanation was a lie, Logan would think up a good one.

Jack quickly closed the chopper door behind them before pointing to a cabinet. "There's food and water over there. Help yourselves. And ma'am, Logan flew in a new baby car seat. He figured you'd have to leave the other one behind during the trek down the mountain."

Logan was thorough and professional and prepared, and he could coordinate hundreds of details, Kirk had to give him that. What other man would remember the baby needed a car seat and would figure out that that piece of gear would, of necessity, be left behind? And every time Jack spoke his boss's name, his utmost respect came through loud and clear. Even without an explanation, Kirk's instincts told him to trust these men, but he needed much more than instinct, with Sara's and Abby's lives on the line.

Pepper curled up in the back of the chopper. Sara removed Abby from the sling and buckled her into the seat. "Give Logan my thanks for the car seat."

"I will, ma'am. But it'll have to wait. Logan's ordered radio silence."

Kirk didn't immediately buckle in. Since no one had appeared to threaten them, he wanted answers—

and now was a good time. "Jack, just what the hell is going on?"

Jack took the pilot's seat and began a preflight check. "Hold on a sec. I'll explain after we take off."

"You'll explain now." Kirk was one second away from pulling out his weapon. But he'd learned the rules of engagement a long time ago. Don't pull a gun unless prepared to shoot. And he couldn't help liking Jack Donovan, who'd put down his own weapon after he'd assured himself of Kirk's identity. The way Jack handled himself, the fact that he'd risked his life to fly Kirk here, elicited trust. But trust only went so far.

"I do owe you an apology." Jack fired up the engine and looked back with a sheepish grin. "See this knot behind my ear? I was flying recon and stopped in my usual spot to answer a call of nature, and got conked over the head—that'll teach me to be so predictable. I woke up to this egg on my head and a long walk back to camp. Someone had stolen my chopper."

Truth or fiction? The man did have a knot the size of a lemon behind his ear. And he sounded embarrassed that he'd been outmaneuvered.

The rotors whirred, and Kirk automatically reached for the headset so they could continue the conversation. He strapped into his seat and handed Sara a headset, too. He believed Jack's story, but now he had more questions.

"How'd you get the chopper back?" Sara asked casually, but from Jack's amused expression, he recognized her suspicion.

Leave it to Sara to ask the crucial question.

"After I got coldcocked, Logan sent out a raiding party." Jack grinned with pleasure. "We stole back our aircraft."

"From whom?"

"That's the sixty-four-thousand dollar question. It appeared to be a one-man operation and the man fled into the woods. Whoever he is—"

"Was."

"—he's good." Jack piloted the chopper smoothly into the air. "Did you say *was?* He's dead?"

"Yeah. I'll give you the coordinates of his body. Maybe Logan can make an ID."

"Was he the same guy who ditched Sara's plane?"

Kirk shook his head.

"Logan believes there's got to be some high-level guy pulling the strings."

"Any proof?"

"Not that I know of, but Logan's hunches are incredibly accurate."

Kirk had to agree. He'd suspected from the start that more than one person was behind the conspiracy to steal Sara's work.

Jack pointed to a compartment. "Open that. Inside is a keyboard that uplinks to encrypted satellite communications."

Automatically, Kirk handed the keyboard to Sara. She followed Jack's instructions, her fingers dancing over the keyboard. "Okay, I'm in."

She typed in the coordinates of the body—a short burst that wouldn't be traceable. "Anything else?"

"Nope." Jack eased the chopper between two mountains. "Logan's already made ten different flight reservations out of Denver to California to cover your tracks.''

"Will we be tailed?'' Kirk asked.

"You never know.''

"Look, I appreciate additional protection and security, but I don't want to shoot or lose the wrong man by accident.''

"It won't happen,'' Jack assured him with such confidence that Kirk dropped the subject.

Then Jack spoke to Sara. "You still have the software?''

"Why?'' Sara asked her voice even, but wary. Clearly she didn't trust Jack Donovan.

"Logan reset your meeting with the government boys for noon tomorrow in Los Angeles.''

Kirk raised his eyebrow. "Logan did this before we took off? Before we contacted him by the satellite uplink?''

"He went to work the moment you showed up in camp the first time to swipe the diapers.''

Kirk knew that getting in and out of that camp unseen had been too easy. However, he couldn't help but grin. He was good in the woods and he'd seen no one. But he could have been tracked with thermal imagers or other classified electronic devices.

"And why didn't Logan come say hello?'' Kirk asked, as he accepted a sandwich and drink from Sara.

"He figured the possibility of someone watching us was too high. Some of the team wanted to go in and help you out after the chopper incident, but Logan insisted that you could get them out by yourself. He didn't want our team to compromise your safety.''

Logan had figured pretty damn well. He'd trusted

Kirk to protect Sara and Abby, to get them safely down the mountain—and he had. Kirk couldn't help being impressed with Logan Kincaid's operation, his leadership or his team. He recalled Logan's offer to join them. A few years ago, he might have jumped at the opportunity, but now, he had other concerns.

Like Sara. And Abby. As they flew toward civilization, he could feel Sara rebuilding the walls he'd torn down. She was pulling away, preparing for him to leave.

While Logan had made plane reservations for *all* of them to go to Los Angeles, Kirk would bet the cash in his pack that sometime soon Sara would suggest they split up in Denver, that he fly back to Michigan. However, Kirk had no intention of leaving Sara and Abby to strangers—he didn't care how good Logan's team was.

If Logan and Kirk both figured that the men might again try to steal Sara's software, then the possibility had to be high. The danger enormous.

IT SEEMED TO SARA that the transition back to civilization occurred almost as quickly as the plane crash. The swift helicopter trip to Denver, followed by a flight to California, gave Sara time to dismantle her computer in the rest room. She hid the hard drive with her program inside her jacket pocket and returned to her seat with her laptop. Although she didn't believe they were being followed, her enemies knew where she was going.

The limo ride to the hotel left her too exhausted to think beyond taking care of Abby. Luckily Logan had planned their itinerary to the nth degree, leaving neither their comfort nor Abby's to chance.

Logan had reserved a hotel suite for them that included three bedrooms, two with king-size beds and private baths, the third with a crib, playpen and stroller for Abby. The suite came stocked with diapers, changes in clothing for all of them, Internet connections and even dog food for Pepper.

Before Sara could say "room service," a maid knocked on the door. A frumpy, peach-shaped middle-aged maid in a form-fitted uniform entered with a cart of linens, stacks of fresh towels and chocolate mints meant for the pillows when she turned down the beds at night.

"I'm Milly and I'll be taking care of your rooms for the next few days. If you want anything, merely call the front desk. Security is guarding the suite, so you folks can relax." The friendly woman handed Kirk a key. "For the minibar."

"Thanks."

Milly carried the towels from her cart into the bathroom. When she returned she spied Abby playing with Pepper. "They're adorable together."

Sara hoped Kirk gave the maid a big tip, though didn't have the energy to even ask. She longed for a shower, but first Abby needed feeding and a bath. Afterward, Sara placed Abby in the crib. The baby cried a little, fussing but not protesting enough for Sara to be concerned.

Smelling lightly of spicy aftershave, Kirk entered the room and picked up Abby, rocking her against his chest. Abby stared at his black hair, damp and curling at the collar after his shower, his jaw smooth from a fresh shave, and hesitantly stopped fussing.

"She sometimes cries just a little before she falls asleep," Sara told him.

"Let me rock her to sleep, Sara. I've already showered, go on and take yours. I'll stay with Abby until she falls asleep."

Sara could tell he really wanted to rock Abby to sleep, and she was too tired to argue. If Kirk wanted to play daddy for a few hours, she saw no harm in his actions. As he reached for their daughter, Abby trusted him, snuggling in his arms and cooing with delight.

"Daddy," Kirk told her. "Say *Daddy,* little girl."

"Good girl?" Abby smiled at him proudly. "Good girl?"

"Da-da," he insisted.

Sara left them to their conversation and headed straight for the bathroom. A huge glass shower stood in one corner, a tub filled with jets in another. Much too dirty to consider soaking, she adjusted the faucets, intending to stand under the hot water for as long as it took to feel clean. The hotel had supplied assorted shampoos, conditioners and soaps. A thick terry robe hung on the back of the door, with slippers nearby.

She shed her clothes and avoided looking into any mirrors. Wanting to wash away days of dirt and sweat and grime before she caught sight of herself, she was grateful for the fog that clouded her reflection.

Sara stepped into the immaculate shower. Letting the hot water sluice over her skin seemed the ultimate luxury. She reached for the shampoo and did a quick wash, fully intending to treat herself to a second, more thorough shampoo. But first she lathered the soap and tackled the top layer of grime. She found a razor and shaved her legs and under her arms, almost feeling human again.

Eyes closed, she was reaching for the shampoo again when the cool air of the open glass door alerted her to Kirk's presence. She opened her eyes and looked at him naked for the first time in almost a year and a half.

"Didn't you already shower?"

"Not with you."

Her pulse fluttered and the moisture in her mouth suddenly disappeared. She recalled running her fingers over his broad chest through crisp curls, enjoying the sensitivity of his nipples responding to a tweak and a nibble. If she reached out and stroked him with her palms, his skin would feel warm and hard, so different from hers and yet so right. And she ached to feel his heart beating sure and strong and swift, making her feel powerful and feminine and very much alive.

Broad-shouldered and muscular, somehow larger and more male than she remembered, he reached for the shampoo, his voice husky. "Let me wash your hair."

She stalled. Why couldn't she just have this one night, enjoy him one more time? They were both single adults. Experience told her that their coming together now would make the separation tomorrow much more difficult. But she wanted him.

She stalled some more. "Abby?"

"She's asleep and Pepper's curled up under her crib."

He shut the shower door behind him, sure of his welcome. Damn him. He knew she wanted him. He'd come to her when she was simply too tired to fight her own needs and him, too. She registered the thought and accepted the consequences in a heartbeat. After almost dying on that mountain, she couldn't deny herself the comfort of his touch or the pleasure of his hands on her body. She craved him. All of him.

A glance at his straining sex told her quite clearly that he wanted her as much as she wanted him. She hadn't made love in so long that the need pounded in her, but she controlled that need with the experience of a woman.

They were two adults who'd made love many times and knew one another's bodies well. Yet the absence of lovemaking for so long kept her trembling with anticipation. Her nipples puckered and moisture beaded between her legs, her physical responses way ahead of her churning emotions.

She'd turned her back to him, giving him easy access to her hair. Kirk had yet to touch her. From her peripheral vision, she watched him pour shampoo into his palm, and then with clever fingers he worked a lather over her scalp.

He leaned close, his chest caressing her back, his hips cradling her bottom. "You smell so good."

"I already washed once," she admitted, groaning as his fingers massaged her head. "I'm not sure I'll ever feel clean again."

"We can stay under the hot water as long as you like. Until your fingertips prune," he teased. "Or until the hotel's hot water runs out."

"Does that happen?"

''You want to find out?''

She tipped her face to the streaming water and rinsed the shampoo from her hair. She began to turn around, but his hand clasped her waist. ''Conditioner?''

She wanted to tell him to screw the conditioner. To screw her, instead. Now that she'd made up her mind to make love, her body had jump-started with a shock to her system that was already building toward orgasm. Kirk had always had this effect on her. He barely needed to touch her before she was raring to attack him, which was why she'd been so careful to keep her distance—but that hadn't worked.

Usually she let him set the pace. But tonight her impatience got the best of her. She turned, lifted her chin and tugged his mouth down for a kiss. Calmly, he nibbled on her lips, while continuing to thread the conditioner through her hair.

She pursed her lips. ''Kiss me, damn you.''

''I am,'' he teased, lightly biting her bottom lip.

Heart thudding in anticipation, she tugged his head closer. ''Harder.''

''Yes, ma'am.''

He kept nibbling.

''Kiss me, Kirk. Hold me tight.''

His arms closed around her, dragging her against him, the slick rinse causing her breasts to slip and slide against his chest in satiny and sensuous circles that elevated her pulse and caused her to rise on tiptoe to anchor her mouth to his. He tasted of toothpaste, smelled of aftershave, felt like paradise.

She wrapped her arms around his neck. ''Making love doesn't mean anything.''

"Right."

She wrapped her legs around his hips. "Tomorrow we go our separate ways."

"Umm."

She reached down to take him inside her. "Making love doesn't change our relationship."

"Uh-huh." He twisted away from her hands. "Hold on a sec." Carrying her, he opened the shower door, reached into the pocket of his robe that was hanging there, pulled out a condom and held it up in triumph.

"Hurry," she demanded, biting his neck, impatient to have him inside her, but not the least bit surprised he'd had the forethought to bring a condom. Whether in the wilds or the bedroom or the shower, Kirk prided himself on his preparation, and she'd come to count on that.

He braced strong legs. "Hold still or I'll never get the package open."

"Here, let me." She released one hand from around his neck and slipped a little. He tried to support her by holding her bottom. Their hands collided, and for a moment she felt the foil packet, then the slippery foil slid between her fingers and fell to the shower floor. She peered over his arm at the still-sealed packet as it swirled toward the drain. "Damn."

He half chuckled, half groaned, then suggested huskily in her ear, "If you would unwrap your legs from my waist, you could climb down and pick up the packet."

Frustration and urgency warred with logic and necessity. "I don't want to let you go."

"And I don't want to make you pregnant. Again."

She rubbed her full breasts against his chest, enjoying the hard feel of him against her sensitive nipples, wondering if she could entice him into changing his mind. "Lactating mothers aren't supposed to ovulate."

He gasped at the sensations she'd created by rubbing against him, but frowned down at her. "Are you saying you *can't* get pregnant?"

Tightening her legs around him for support, she reached for his sex, attempting to put him inside her. "I'm saying another pregnancy is unlikely at this time."

"I'm not taking that chance."

"Fine." She loved it when he went all protective on her. She cocked her head, challenging him. "And I'm not letting go."

"Then I...have two...choices." He spoke from between gritted teeth. "I can try to lower us to the floor...without falling."

"Or?"

"I can carry you...into the bedroom...where I have more condoms."

"Your choice." She bit his shoulder as cold water rained down her back. "However, you might want to hurry."

"Why is that?"

"We just ran out of hot water."

She opened the shower door. He cupped his hands under her bottom and stalked into the bedroom next to the room where the baby slept in her crib. Abby didn't make a peep, and Pepper didn't come to investigate—even after Kirk toppled Sara onto the bed and she shrieked.

"You're getting the covers all wet."

"So I'll sleep in your room."

"Who said anything about sleep?" She looked over his shoulder to the open box on the nightstand. "You only have five condoms?"

He grinned at her, then ripped open a packet. "If we get desperate, there's still one left on the bathroom floor."

Heat burned through her. She wanted her hands back on his flesh, her mouth on his. "Will you quit talking and put that on already?"

"For someone so slow to make up her mind, you're certainly in one big hurry."

Impatient, she took the condom and rolled it over him. "It's been a long time. And I've never been the patient type." She yanked him onto his back, then straddled him.

"Wait." His hands clasped her hips, holding her perfectly still.

She sighed in exasperation. "Now what?"

"I want to look at you."

She rolled her eyes, impatient to sheath him inside her. "You already know what I look like."

"The water droplets are making your skin glisten."

"That's great." She shifted her hips, but he held her steady, open, ready for him, but he wasn't cooperating.

"And your breasts are—"

"Cold." She could play this game. Leaning forward until her nipple brushed his lips, she teased him, taunted him, enjoying the feminine power of eliciting his soft groan. "You could warm me up."

He pleasured her with his tongue. And he released

her hips, the fingers of one hand delving between her thighs, but still preventing her from lowering herself onto him. His fingers parted her, slipped into aching, hungry flesh. And he held her on the edge between anticipation and bliss, seeking to explore every slick inch of her.

His explorations lit a match to her already over-heated state. Her muscles kindled and fired. And as if sensing the flaming moment of her orgasm, he thrust inside her, allowing her to blaze around him. But he didn't pause to allow her burning senses to cool. He gave her no rest, thrusting his hips in, filling her, then drawing back before she caught her breath, creating a raging heat.

Fast-paced and furious, she rode him with uninhibited joy. She had no doubts, no regrets, simply took what he gave her and enjoyed the ride. And all the while, his resourceful fingers urged her on, caressing all her sensitive places, applying exactly the right amount of pressure that only married couples who'd made love to one another for years could know so well.

And Kirk had forgotten nothing. He recalled what and how and where she liked to be touched, driving her close to madness, before she succumbed again, exploding. And again he held back, giving her no time to rest or recover, pushing her beyond the plateau she'd just reached, urging her toward the peak of fulfillment.

Trusting him, she ignored the roaring in her ears. Blood singing through her veins. Her pulse soaring until she couldn't think of anything but more friction. Gyrating her hips, she clutched his shoulders and let her movements go wild. Together they spiraled, and when release came again, this time they climaxed together.

She bit back a scream and collapsed atop him, straightening her legs and pillowing her head on his shoulder but keeping him inside her. And with release came the reawakening of emotions she didn't want to face.

She loved this man. She'd loved him as a young girl. She'd loved him as a married woman. She loved him still.

He held her tight, but not too tight. His voice was raw and awed. "The room's spinning."

"I have faith that you'll make a full recovery."

But *she* wouldn't. She'd divorced him, believing that he would never change his career. While he *had* left the military, she didn't ever want to pin her hopes on his survival again—not with the constant danger he put himself in.

Loving him made hope for a future much too painful. But she'd spent the past almost year and a half attempting to convince herself that their marriage hadn't been that strong. That loving him hadn't been so great.

She'd been fooling herself. But was waiting almost a year and a half to hold him again in her arms worth all the pain of separation? Now that she'd again been branded by his heat, she didn't know if she could find the courage to say goodbye.

However, she had promised herself tonight. And tonight was far from over. As soon as she recovered a little strength, she intended to make up for lost time.

Tomorrow morning would come all too soon.

Chapter Eleven

Kirk slept heavily and awakened slowly. With Logan's team providing extra security, he'd gotten the first good hours of rest in days. From the sunlight streaming through the hotel windows, he estimated the time at mid-morning. Stretching out assorted aches in muscles he'd overtaxed, he spied the empty condom packets scattered over the nightstand and grinned. While he supposed the hotel maid had seen the evidence of lovemaking before, he preferred to keep their activities private, so he picked up the wrappers and deposited them in the wastebasket.

Last night with Sara had been incredible. Not just physically, either. Although neither of them had seemed able to get enough of the other, she'd touched him emotionally in ways that had helped him heal, making him feel more alive than he had since their divorce.

Before coming to rescue Sara, he'd forced himself to make plans for his future, but for the first time, he looked forward to the days ahead, and the difference in attitude lightened his steps.

Since his divorce, Kirk had known he had a hollow

spot in his heart and had figured that eventually time would dull the ache. He hadn't realized how easily Sara could fill him up with joy. And love. Yes, they'd shared love last night. He knew Sara well enough to be sure that she wouldn't have gone along with his seduction unless she cared deeply for him, too.

Her love helped eased the pain of their long separation and gave him hope for a future together. Bending back over the bed, Kirk felt the mattress for her warmth, wondering how long ago she'd awakened.

The sheets were cold.

Where was she? Ordering breakfast from room service? Perhaps Abby had awakened, and Sara had gone to feed her. If so, he wanted to watch.

Slipping on a robe, he knotted the sash and padded from one bedroom to another. He found Sara in his room, packing his things.

Had Logan decided they should vacate the hotel?

Puzzled, slightly fuzzy from the strenuous night of lovemaking, Kirk glanced from Sara, busy stuffing a shirt into his pack, to Pepper and Abby playing on the floor. With a chuckle, Abby threw her toys and Pepper brought them back.

Kirk took the pack from Sara. "What's up?"

The moment she saw him, she paled. Her lips trembled, then tightened as if she had received bad news but wanted to put on a brave front.

He rubbed his jaw, trying not to jump to conclusions. "If something's wrong, you should have wakened me. Did Logan phone? Is the security gone? Are you in danger?"

She shook her head. "The security team is standing

guard right outside the door. We're safe. And my face-recognition program's well hidden—''

So why had he glimpsed tears pooling in her eyes before she fought them down. ''Last night…''

''What about last night?'' Surely he hadn't been too rough. She had matched him move for move, urging him to last longer, go harder. One look at the expression in her eyes and his gut twisted. Something was very wrong and he didn't have a clue what.

Her voice cracked. ''Last night. I'll always remember…as special.''

She was sending him away.

He didn't know why, but he could see the message in her eyes, read it in the slump of her shoulders and the determined tilt of her chin.

She was sending him away.

Sara might as well have rapped him on the skull with a crowbar. Pain exploded behind his eyes. His stomach churned. He wanted to strike out and hit something. But he didn't flinch. Willed himself to think.

Kirk knew how to fight his enemies, knew how to focus on his goals. But he had no weapons to fight the woman he loved. Not when she didn't want him anymore.

He hadn't seen her reaction coming, but he should have. This was normal for her. His lack of foresight filled him with anger. Of course she was trying to push him away. He'd gotten too close. And she wanted to run.

''I love you, Sara.''

She folded her arms over her chest. ''Love isn't enough. Last night…was wonderful and foolish. But

I can't set myself up for heartache again. I can't stand by like the good little woman, while you go on dangerous missions. Knowing that you're in danger tears me apart.''

"I've given that up."

"Have you? Have you turned down Logan's job offer?"

"I have the ranch..."

"Land that you lease is not permanent." She sighed. "I promised myself I would live with the consequences of last night. Well, unfortunately, you're going to have to live with them, too." She trembled and stood, her spine rigid, as if ready to snap. "I'm sorry."

"Sorry?"

"I was weak last night."

"Wrong. Last night you were strong. Last night you reached out for what you wanted with courage. And let's be clear. You wanted me, Sara. This morning your courage has vanished, so you're sending me away."

"You're right."

Her words dissolved his anger and left him defeated. How could he argue with a woman who agreed with him? More importantly, how could he change her mind?

He couldn't think of a way. Sara's mind worked so differently from his, it was a wonder they got along as well as they did. As well as they *had*.

She was sending him away.

Quitting wasn't part of a Marine's psyche. Yet Sara wasn't giving him a choice. Besides, he wouldn't stay with a woman who didn't want him. And he wouldn't beg.

Realizing that now was not the time to discuss Abby's custody, he hefted the bag onto his shoulder, prepared to walk out of the suite.

"Kirk." Sara's voice was choked and she wouldn't look him in the eye, but stared over his left shoulder.

On his way to the door, he paused. "Yeah."

Sara brushed away a stray tear. "You might want to take a minute to change your clothes."

Kirk looked down. Sara wasn't the only upset adult in the room. He was stilling wearing his bathrobe.

AFTER KIRK SHUT THE DOOR behind him, Sara collapsed onto the bed, burst into tears and hugged the pillow to her chest. The suite seemed empty and cold without his presence, just like her heart. She'd known sending him away would be hard. But she hadn't expected his departure to feel as if she'd swallowed glassy shards of despair.

She told herself that prolonging his departure would have made her feel worse, but, in truth, she didn't know how she could feel much worse than she did right now.

Already, she missed him terribly. And guilt filled her for the pain she'd caused them both.

While she hadn't asked him to rescue her from that mountain, she *had* invited him into her bed last night. Deep down she knew he might be the only man she would ever love. So she had to remind herself that keeping him close hurt worse than keeping him at a distance.

She recalled all too well how depressed she'd been

when he'd lived in danger every day. She couldn't take the pressure. And knowing that other women did somehow find the inner strength to let the men they loved go into life-threatening situations only made her feel like a failure. Cops, firemen and military people all had higher divorce rates than average citizens. The pressures were enormous—not just because of the endless separations. She couldn't cope with Kirk's way of life—and didn't believe he could really change.

He'd said he had quit the military for good, but he was considering taking other dangerous missions. And that ranch sounded more like a dream than reality. He could pack up and leave at a moment's notice for a stranger in trouble, the same way he'd done to come after her.

Sara had lived under that kind of cloud for too many years and, when she'd divorced Kirk, she'd done so to survive and to preserve her sanity. She'd divorced him before he could damage their baby by his long absences. Her decision might not have been fair, but it was right for her.

Still, that didn't make his exit any less devastating. It didn't mean that tonight she wouldn't roll over in bed and reach for him. Last night had given her precious memories that she would file away with so many others. The first time they'd made love. Her honeymoon. The night of Abby's conception. And now the final goodbye.

Sara strode into the bathroom and washed away her tears. She brought a cold, wet washcloth to her red eyes, hoping the swollen evidence of her tears would recede before her meeting. She needed to calm herself and feed Abby, whom she intended to take with her.

If the Department of Defense men didn't like her bringing the baby, that was tough. No way would she leave Abby with a stranger, not after their harrowing experiences of the past few days.

"Hello?" The maid called out, interrupting Sara's thoughts. "I've brought fresh towels."

The maid had probably knocked, but Sara hadn't heard her over the sink's running water. "Just leave the towels on the bed. Abby's asleep in her playpen, so don't go in that room, either. Okay?"

"Whatever you say, ma'am."

Sara needed to pull herself together. She had three hours before her meeting. She needed to shower, fix her hair and put on makeup, feed the baby and dress them both for the meeting. Thanks to Logan Kincaid, she had everything she needed. Clothes, diapers, a stroller. He'd even sent an armored limo with security. She and Abby would be quite safe.

And since Sara didn't trust her own computer to run her program, she was grateful for Logan's thoughtfulness. The man had spared no expense to make her and the baby comfortable. Too bad not even Logan Kincaid had a cure for her broken heart.

She supposed Logan knew, from the security detail guarding her, that Kirk had left. She shoved the stomach-roiling subject from her mind. In three hours, she could put this incident behind her. She would have secured Abby's future, and the government would have a powerful new program for Homeland Security.

Once she sold the program to the government, any danger would be over. She had nothing to worry about. Unless the hard drive had been damaged during the plane crash. Unless the hard drive had frozen. Unless she had damaged the hardware when she'd hastily removed it from the case. After abusing her battery by starting that spark to keep them alive during the blizzard, she hadn't dared to fire up the machine to run her program.

Sara stepped into the connecting bedroom to check on Abby. She was sleeping soundly in her crib. No doubt she wouldn't be pleased to awaken and find her new best friend, Pepper, gone.

Abby sighed and returned to her shower. At least Abby could easily be distracted. At nine months, a baby didn't have a long memory. Her daughter wouldn't spend the next weeks, months and years yearning for her father—not like Sara would.

Sara refused to think about joint custody or paternal visits. She wanted to rinse the memories of Kirk down the drain and clear her mind for the meeting.

She stepped under the water, remembering her last shower. Kirk's hands in her hair. The scent of his male body. His gentle fingertips massaging her scalp. His clever mouth nipping and…

Stop.

She couldn't keep torturing herself or she would go mad. Kirk was gone. She just needed to pretend this past week had never happened. She had to reset her internal emotional clock back to the week before, when he'd been a painful memory, not a bleeding and agonizing wound.

Not for the first time, she wished he hadn't been so good at what he did. His animals practically read his mind. And the world would always come to his door, asking too much of him.

Stop. Think about your meeting.

But all she could think about was the hurt in Kirk's eyes, the shock on his face when he'd realized that she wanted him to go. She told herself he should have known that sex wouldn't change her mind. Not even good sex. Okay, spectacular sex.

No, she couldn't fool herself. They hadn't just had sex, they'd made love.

Swallowing past the tightness in her throat, she finished her shower and wrapped herself in a towel, her wet hair twisted under a turban. She had a powerful urge to hold Abby, but she needed the time to dry her hair, apply makeup and dress before waking her baby for one last feeding before they headed to the hotel lobby.

Abby refused to look at the rumpled sheets on the bed where Kirk had held her so tenderly. She strode to the closet and removed the business suit, blouse and shoes Logan had supplied. The man knew how to shop. She'd never have bought anything so exquisite. He'd gotten her size correct, right down to soft, leather shoes. If the sale of her program went through, she knew she could buy a dozen suits and a closet full of shoes.

Sara sighed and dressed. What she wanted most couldn't be bought with cold cash. Money had never been Kirk's priority and Sara hadn't minded one bit. She'd loved his dedication, his heart, his pride in what he did. And she'd always known that asking him to give up that life was wrong. When she'd finally broken down and asked, he'd refused, hurting her more than she could bear.

As if programmed in a closed-circuit logic loop, her mind always circled back to him. She didn't want to think about him, and yet she couldn't seem to help herself.

She sat in front of a cosmetic table and, with shaking fingers, applied foundation, mascara, lipstick and blush—all compliments of Logan Kincaid. Although his specialty was computers, whenever his name came up, rumors always flew. Especially about Logan's women. The man knew women, what they liked and what they needed. He also had one of the most brilliant minds she'd ever encountered.

But she wasn't attracted to Logan.

Why was it that only Kirk Hardaker could set her on fire with a glance? Why couldn't she drum up interest in someone else? Sometimes she thought that her and Kirk's long history kept them connected—but she hadn't thought once about history when he'd held her last night.

Sara glanced at her watch. Time to wake and feed Abby. She couldn't wait to hold her, cuddle her small body against her aching heart.

Opening the door, she peeked into the darkened room. She'd have thought Abby would have awakened on her own by now.

Sara slid her hand along the wall and flipped the light switch. Automatically, her gaze focused on the crib.

An empty crib.

KIRK STRODE INTO THE AIRPORT with Pepper, determined to catch the first plane back to Michigan. Sara didn't want him and he intended to go home to lick his wounds and plan his next move.

When his cell phone rang, he answered automatically. "Kirk here."

"Abby's gone."

The panic in Sara's voice had his feet changing direction and heading back to the airport exit before he'd stopped to consider any other response. Pepper trotted alongside him, the loyal animal's ears perking up, immediately sensing something was wrong.

Kirk hadn't thought his stomach could clench any tighter, but he was wrong. It knotted into one massive cramp. And as he breathed in the California smog outside, his breath hitched, sticking in his throat.

"What happened?"

Sara's voice was a whisper of misery. "I checked on Abby soon after you left, and she was sleeping soundly in her crib. After I showered and went in to feed her…she wasn't there."

Kirk had to ask, although he was sure Abby had already done a thorough search. "Could she have climbed out of the crib?"

"Logan's team searched the entire suite, every cabinet, every closet, even looked under the beds. She's gone, Kirk. Our baby's gone." Sara spoke quickly and quietly, but he couldn't miss the raw agony in her tone.

His heart knotted as he heard her terror. "Hang tight, Sara. I'll be back within thirty minutes. In the meantime, do exactly as Logan's men suggest."

Kirk hailed a cab and sped back the way he'd come. At midday the L.A. traffic allowed a decent pace, but it still seemed like a crawl to him. The bright sunshine mocked him. So did people going about their normal lives while he was caught in a nightmare.

Kirk was accustomed to walking into danger. But he felt totally unprepared for the emotional impact of losing his innocent baby to a kidnapper.

He'd barely gotten to know his daughter, but he already loved her.

He couldn't let his emotions rule. Abby and Sara needed him to think clearly. And he didn't care what it took, he would find his baby and bring her back.

How had her enemies found Sara again? The damn government meeting. For all he knew, the information was posted on a Web site. Or someone from the government might be in collusion with the kidnapper. The important thing was that they'd known to look for Sara in Los Angeles because that's where she had to come to sell her software.

His baby was gone and Sara had sounded ready to crack. Sara had doted on their daughter with a maternal instinct he hadn't suspected she'd had. He recalled her proud expression whenever the baby spoke or laughed or tried to stand, recalled the love on her face as she'd breast-fed the child. As bad as he felt, she had to be feeling a hundred times worse.

And poor little Abby. The baby would wake up among strangers in a place she didn't recognize. She might be terrified. And when Abby was unhappy, she cried. Loudly.

Which could draw attention to her presence, but could also irritate her kidnapper. *Hang on, Abby.*

Daddy's coming to get you and bring you home. I promise.

Kirk had to stop wallowing in his emotions. He'd be no good to Sara or Abby if he didn't pull himself together. Slowly, he tamped down the emotions and began analyzing the situation rationally.

How had they gotten inside the suite, and why had they taken Abby? All along, someone had been after Sara's software. Neither of them had ever suspected that their child could be in danger. Kirk recalled the guards posted outside the suite and wondered if they'd been overpowered. He'd know soon enough.

He entered the hotel lobby at a run and rode the elevator straight to Sara's suite. Two guards outside her door let him through without any hassles.

Logan gestured for him to join a group of men, and Sara, who ran and wrapped her arms around him the moment he stepped inside the room. Pale faced, her eyes red and swollen, Sara held him tight. He patted her back in a soothing gesture.

"We're going to find her. She's going to be okay."

Even as he consoled Sara, Kirk assessed Logan's team. He already recognized the helicopter pilot, Jack Donovan, and Logan introduced the other men.

"Ryker Stevens is ex-Special Forces, our business specialist. You met him on the radio during the chopper ride."

Ryker nodded. Ryker possessed strong, forceful features and exhibited intense concentration as he typed furiously onto his laptop's keyboard.

Logan clapped the man on the shoulder. "Ryker specializes in unraveling the intricacies of complicated white-collar crimes. He's trying to trace a pay-off from the kidnapper to the maid.''

Kirk raised a brow. ''The maid?''

Sara finally released him and took a step back. ''We think two maids switched places and the new one took Abby out of here in her laundry cart.''

''Her name is Gail Fennway and she's worked here for twenty years.'' The next man on the team spoke from the sofa. He sat quite still with a cell phone plastered to each ear, but told Kirk about the maid as if accustomed to carrying on three conversations at the same time. His pager kept beeping, and he handled the multitasking with ease, acknowledging Kirk's presence with a sharp nod.

Logan gestured to the cell phone addict. ''Web Garfield is ex-CIA. He's the one who's been protecting your back.''

Kirk took in Web Garfield's casual demeanor but wasn't fooled. Web kept himself in top-notch condition, his shirt stretching over a muscular chest and powerful arms, the telltale ridges and calluses on the ex-agent's hands revealing that he excelled in deadly hand-to-hand combat.

Ryker frowned at his computer screen. ''Gail Fennway deposited one hundred grand into her bank account half an hour ago.''

''Can you trace the check back to the depositor?'' Web asked, again, putting his multiple-phone conversations on hold.

Ryker shook his head. ''The wire transfer came from out of the country. The Cayman Islands. Gail withdrew the cash and purchased a money order made out to L.A. Memorial Hospital.''

Web stood. "I'm on it."

"Hold on." Logan held up his hand. "Let Ryker see if she's checked in as a patient." While the man typed and Web murmured into his phones, Logan strode over to the last man in the group. "This is Travis Cantrel, an expert in hostage negotiations."

Sara's eyes widened. Kirk wrapped an arm over her shoulder and could feel her trembling in distress.

Travis looked like a wrestler. He had a barrel chest, rounded shoulders and legs as thick as telephone poles. He spoke with a Texas drawl, and a diamond winked in his ear. "I'm expecting the kidnappers to call soon and demand a ransom," he said.

Web stared at the computer screen over Ryker's shoulder. "Don't crowd me," Ryker complained. "The hospital has a firewall that's on the touchy side."

Web took a half step back. "I need to move now. Call me with—"

A knock on the door startled Sara. Web reached for a weapon. Ryker kept typing, and Logan turned casually but kept his back to a wall. Travis didn't move a muscle, the diamond in his ear shining brightly. Kirk led Sara toward the sofa, wanting her to sit before she collapsed. The stress on her face made his heart ache.

The security guard poked his head through the doorway. "Sir, there's a woman out here you need to talk with."

"What's her name?" Logan asked.

"Gail Fennway. She claims to have information about the baby, sir."

"The maid?" Sara tugged on Jack's sleeve. "We have to talk to her."

"Easy now. Don't attack her," Kirk warned.

The security guard returned to the hallway, patted down the woman, then spoke through the open door. "She's clean."

Logan nodded at Web. The man stepped into a doorway and merged with the shadows. Travis did the same on the other side. Ryker kept typing. "There's no Gail Fennway at L.A. Memorial. No other Fennways, either. Our gal's got a clean record except for two speeding tickets twenty years ago. Her credit card is maxed out. And the bank's about to foreclose on her trailer. A secondhand dealer repo-ed her car last week."

The woman had money problems, but so did lots of people. Jack wondered if she knew that kidnapping was a felony and that if she was convicted she'd end up behind bars for the rest of her life. Most criminals disappeared after the payoff. They didn't come out of the woodwork to shake down their victims.

Gail Fennway hurried into the room, wringing her hands, mascara leaking from her eyelashes down her wrinkled cheeks, her white hair a mess. She didn't have the record of a criminal and she didn't act like one. She looked guilty and full of remorse.

She rushed toward Sara and Kirk. "I'm so sorry."

Sara started to approach the kidnapper, but Kirk held her back where he could protect her if the woman pulled a weapon.

Sara jerked free of his grip. "Where's Abby? What have you done with my baby?"

Chapter Twelve

Sara stared at Gail waiting for an answer, her teeth clenched. Anger raged through her so furiously that she shook. Never in her life had she wanted to hurt anyone. Until now. It took every fiber of her self-control not to attack the woman.

How could Gail have taken her child? Sara had read about child kidnappings in the newspaper, seen parents' desperate faces on television and had always felt sorry for those involved, but she'd never expected such trauma to happen to her.

And she had so many worries circling through her mind, she had trouble concentrating. She couldn't stop thinking that somehow Abby's disappearance was all her fault. She should have kept the baby with her every second, never let her out of her sight. She should have hired a security specialist to stand guard over her crib, or canceled the meeting and backed out of selling the face-recognition program—anything to have Abby back and safe in her arms.

Gail burst into tears. "It wasn't supposed to happen this way."

Logan placed a hand on the distraught woman's

arm and led her to a chair, where she collapsed into sobs. She took a tissue from her pocket and dabbed her eyes.

"I'm sorry. So sorry."

"Tell us what happened," Logan suggested gently. The man was the epitome of caring.

Sara wanted to shake the words out of the woman, but held onto just enough of her sanity to recognize that Logan's technique would elicit more information. Kirk's steadying arm over Sara's shoulder lent her enough support to dig deep for control.

The moment she'd realized Abby was missing that morning, her first instinct had been to call Kirk. And now she was more than glad to have him at her side. But she couldn't help wondering if Kirk had to fight back the same violent tendencies that welled up in her.

Gail's mascara ran down her cheeks with her tears. "I needed the money."

"You risked my child's life for money?" Sara snapped, hearing her voice rise an octave.

More tears brimmed in Gail's eyes. "She was supposed to stay with me. I intended to keep her safe."

Sara's heart ached and so did her breasts. Without Abby to remove the milk, she was swollen and uncomfortable. In the baby supplies that Logan had bought—that man thought of every detail—he'd supplied a breast pump. She would excuse herself to use it at the first opportunity.

"Could we please start at the beginning," Logan said quietly, but Sara heard the steely tone of an order beneath his polite request.

Gail blew her nose noisily into the tissue. "A man

phoned and promised me a hundred thousand dollars if I would steal your computer.''

Ryker poised his hands over the keyboard. ''Do you know the man's name?''

She shook her head.

Ryker stroked his keyboard but didn't press any keys. ''When exactly did he call?''

''Two days ago at eight o'clock.''

Ryker started typing. ''He probably called from a pay phone, but I'll check with the phone company.''

Sara suspected he might not have permission to hack into the phone company's database, but she didn't care. It wasn't as if Ryker would do any harm, and he might get them a lead.

''My computer isn't missing, my daughter is,'' Sara reminded the woman.

''I took your computer to a man waiting in the next room down the hall, but he said the information they wanted wasn't there.''

Sara had been right to keep the hard drive hidden. But she realized with a sick feeling in her gut that if they'd found the program, they wouldn't have taken her baby. ''So they convinced you to kidnap my child, instead?''

''I knew you'd be upset—''

Upset? Sara wanted to deck this woman, but antagonizing their only lead would be stupid.

''—and after they called me the second time with the plan to take your child, I decided I could live with my conscience if I took very good care of your baby.''

''What did the man you met look like?'' Logan asked.

"I don't know. The drapes were pulled in the hotel room, and he didn't turn on a light. He was taller than me, that's all I can say."

Logan spoke quietly. "This man ordered you to return the computer and grab the baby?"

"Yes."

"Then what?"

"I was supposed to go to my bank, verify that the money was deposited and take the baby to a safe place."

"You went to the bank?"

"Yes. And I paid the hospital the money for my grandchild's bone-marrow transplant." Gail gazed with teary eyes at Sara. "She's only ten and will die without the operation. Insurance wouldn't cover the procedure since they claim it's experimental. I needed the money to save her life."

Sara steeled herself against the woman's sad story. "And you risked my child in the process?"

"There wasn't *supposed* to be any risk."

"Why?" Sara challenged her.

"I would have taken good care of the baby and returned her to you. I didn't even want to make you worry, but when I weighed my granddaughter's life against your worry, I just thought…"

"Where is my daughter?" Sara asked again, her stomach sick.

"I don't know. The moment I walked out of the bank, a stranger stole her from me."

"Can you describe him?" Logan asked.

"Tall. White. Middle-aged with brown hair. He wore black pants and a black coat. He could have been the same man I met in the hotel room, but I can't be certain.''

Ryker stopped typing. ''The call was made from a pay phone at the airport. It's unlikely anyone will remember the person using the phone.''

''You don't usually clean this suite, do you?'' Logan asked the maid.

Gail shook her head. ''I asked to be switched here. It was easy to do since Milly, the attendant who usually works this shift, didn't show up today.''

''I'm on it,'' Ryker muttered and started typing. ''What's her full name?''

''Milly Pane.'' Gail's eyes suddenly widened in terror. ''You think she's okay, don't you?''

Ryker must have gotten her phone number, because he dialed a cell phone, spoke into it and then hung up. ''She's fine. She had car trouble this morning.''

Logan's phone rang and he spoke quietly, then turned to Ryker. ''Fingerprints from AFIS have identified the body we extracted on the mountain. Complete details are being sent by attachment.''

''Who was he?'' Kirk asked.

Ryker typed at his keyboard and pulled up the incoming data. ''Donald Ely.'' His fingers danced. ''Give me a sec.''

While he researched, Logan escorted Gail from the room, turning her over to the police, who must have been summoned by the security guards. Sara knew she should feel sorry for the woman, but she couldn't—not with Abby's life in danger.

They waited for Ryker to get the information, and Sara excused herself to go to the bathroom and use the breast pump. The slightly painful procedure took half an hour. Exhausted, Sara returned to the living area to hear Ryker's news.

He read the information on his screen. "Donald Ely. Last known address: Ann Arbor, Michigan."

Both she and Kirk were from Michigan, too. A coincidence?

"Ann Arbor is the home city of two of my competitors," Sara told them.

Logan pushed a pad of paper and pen in her direction. "I want the names of the firms, along with their addresses and owners, if you know them."

She knew the names of both men. Educated, professional people like herself didn't kidnap children, make planes fall out of the sky or steal software, did they?

Ryker read them the pertinent information from his lightning-fast search. "Donald Ely's bank account shows another hundred-thousand-dollar deposit that came in last week by wire transfer from the Cayman Islands."

Ryker was truly a wonder at hacking. But maybe Logan's team had clearance and passwords. More likely he'd already found cracks at these sites and had hidden the encryption programs until needed. The method was similar to hiding a key to a lock and finding that key again when one needed to unlock a door.

"Are we talking about the same Cayman bank that Gail's money came from, as well as the same amount of money?" Logan asked.

Sara's hopes rose while Ryker did more fast typing. If Ryker could trace the account, they might learn the identity of Abby's kidnapper. However, she told herself not to get too excited. Even after they identified the kidnapper, they had to find him and somehow rescue Abby.

"Same bank. I can't give you the account number yet. Give me a few minutes."

A few minutes to hack into a Cayman bank? Past the most elaborate security systems created by man or machine? Past the firewalls and encryptions and code? Ryker was damn good at his job, and Sara prayed he would find the information they needed in time to rescue her baby.

"Any chance Ely served as a marine?" Kirk asked, obviously remembering her comment about how the two men had fought with the same skills back on the mountain.

"He was dishonorably discharged two years ago," Ryker told him, then frowned at his screen. "We've got a problem, boss."

"You can't get in?" Logan's voice rose, more in mild surprise than concern. And while she appreciated the smooth efficiency of his team and the superb capabilities of these men, she couldn't help wondering how high the odds were of seeing her baby again.

Ryker leaned back in his chair, cracked his knuckles and swigged down one of those high-caffeine sodas that made Sara's stomach revolt. "This bank is part of the International World Monetary Fund. I've got a crack through a back door that will break security, but my hack will crash the site and shut them down. Maybe create an international incident and panic in the worldwide markets." Ryker looked to Logan for instructions. "It's only fifty-fifty whether I can grab the intel we want before the site crashes. I'll need clearance."

"I'll see what I can do." The team leader strode into a spare bedroom, his phone to his ear.

Sara had finished writing down the information about her competitors, and handed her notes to Ryker. "After you do the background investigations, could you cross-check for connections between these men and Ely?"

"Sure, but it may take some time."

"Good idea," Kirk told Sara, discreetly glancing at his watch. "We're going to get her back. We should receive a ransom call soon."

Sara didn't have such optimism. Maybe she couldn't think past her fear for Abby. And trying so hard to hold herself together took more energy than she would have believed.

The hotel's phone rang.

Adrenaline surged through her like a lightning bolt. She lunged for the receiver, but Web, the ex-CIA agent moved so fast that his hands were a blur, and beat her to it.

"Wait," Web cautioned. "You don't want to seem too eager."

The phone rang again, drawing her nerves taut.

Kirk looked at Web and then glanced at the equipment plugged into the phone. "I'm assuming you will have all calls to this phone recorded and traced?"

Web nodded. "The boss got a judge's order for a wiretap ten minutes after the baby disappeared."

The phone rang again.

Travis Cantrel, the hostage negotiator, spoke for the first time since he'd been introduced to them. His

tone was supportive but firm. "Sara, pretend you are
alone. Make the caller repeat himself. Keep him talking for as long as possible to give our equipment time
to trace the call. Ask to speak to Abby."

With a reassuring hand, Kirk lifted Sara's chin.
"You can do this."

"Okay," she agreed, trembling as she picked up
the phone. Please, please let her do this right. Let her
daughter be safe. She knew that everyone in the room
could hear both sides of the conversation through the
speaker the team had attached to her phone. "Hello?"

The kidnapper's voice sounded as though he spoke
through a machine, like a robot, which effectively dis-
guised his voice. "Mrs. Hardaker?"

"Yes." Every atom in her body urged her to shout
questions into the phone. But Sara couldn't let her
fear interfere with getting back her baby. She spoke
slowly. "Just a minute. I have to put the orange juice
back in the fridge."

"Lady, quit stalling."

"Excuse me. I couldn't understand what you just
said."

Travis signaled her with a thumbs-up. Kirk rubbed
her shoulders, but the tension had her every muscle
hard and knotted and cramped.

"Understand this. If you want to see your baby
alive, you will hand over the software to me. And I
want to see it work."

A chill shimmied down her back. "Okay."

The computer code was the least of her worries.
She'd give up every idea she owned to secure Abby's
release. "Can I talk to Abby?"

"You'll get your daughter—"

"Please."

"—when I get what I asked for. I'll be in touch."

The line went dead. She sank onto the couch in despair, feeling as though the lifeline to Abby had just been cut. The kidnapper hadn't set up a meeting place or a time to exchange the baby for the program. She was sure the short call couldn't be traced in the brief amount of time that she'd kept him talking.

Travis squeezed her shoulder. "You did your best."

Failure didn't sit well in her gut. "My best wasn't good enough."

Web spoke kindly. "Don't beat yourself up over it."

Travis also tried to reassure her. "This guy is technology savvy. He knew the high probability of the call being traced and would have cut the call short no matter what you said."

Web and Travis exchanged glances. "You notice he didn't even warn her not to contact the authorities."

"I noticed," Travis said.

"And what does that mean?" Sara asked.

"Probably nothing, ma'am," Travis told her.

Sara deliberately sharpened her tone. "Do I need to remind you that my daughter's life is at stake?"

"No, ma'am."

"Then, tell me the truth."

Travis didn't look happy that she had cornered him. And his chauvinistic attitude made her angry, even after Kirk nodded for Travis to tell her the truth. Like she needed Kirk to give permission. But now was not the time to quibble. She wanted answers.

Travis spoke with care. "Either the man is stupid and didn't remember to warn you away from the authorities—"

"And this guy is not stupid," Web added.

"—or, he knows we are here."

Kirk frowned. "You mean, there's a leak coming from your end of the operation?"

"Not necessarily—but we do have security around you," Web replied calmly. "And the kidnapper knew that Sara had a meeting set in Los Angeles. With the right resources, putting the information together and finding you wasn't impossibly difficult."

"Bingo." Ryker spoke slowly from the other side of the room, but she couldn't miss his undertone of excitement as he peered at his computer screen. "The dead man on the mountain served in the Marines with Garth Davis—"

Sara gasped.

Kirk's brows drew together. "You recognize the name?"

Ryker spoke and typed at the same time. "I'm e-mailing his picture to the police station. Maybe Gail can identify him as the man who took the baby from her."

Sara stood, suddenly too agitated to sit. She paced in front of the coffee table and explained. "Garth Davis is my competitor. His firm's in Ann Arbor."

Web stood with his back to the wall, a deep frown of concentration furrowing his forehead. "While I don't believe in coincidences, we need to establish a stronger connection than matching hundred-grand bank deposits and old Marine Corps ties. Lots of men served together."

Ryker kept typing. "I'm searching. This may take a while. Usually I follow the money trail, but Garth's banking habits are unusual. His primary bank doesn't show enough cash flow to run a major company, so his major assets must be elsewhere."

"Let me guess," Kirk said as he petted Pepper. "Garth uses international banks. Perhaps one in the Cayman Islands?"

Ryker shook his head. "Switzerland."

Logan reentered the room, his expression stoic. "The head of Homeland Security would prefer we didn't create an international incident." Logan Kincaid had friends in high places, but apparently even they couldn't help them. Logan shifted his gaze to focus on Sara and Kirk. "We'll have to find your daughter another way."

How? Sara wondered. Although these men appeared to have the skills needed, perhaps they should call in the FBI. However, she didn't make the suggestion aloud. Number one, she didn't want to insult these men. And number two, she knew that a wider scope of investigation caused more red tape. Valuable time could be lost communicating and verifying the information they already had and bringing the new people up to speed. Time was critical. She didn't even want to think about what might happen to Abby if the kidnapper panicked.

"We have another complication." Ryker threw out the news and Sara restrained a groan.

She braced herself and could tell Kirk did the same as he came to her side and took her hand, squeezing lightly to lend her courage. She was fresh out. Fear rose up and threatened to overwhelm her. She could barely focus on the conversation.

Get a hold of yourself. Listen to Ryker. He needs your input.

"John Wayne is vacationing in the Cayman Islands right now," Ryker told her.

"John Wayne?" Kirk's eyebrow lifted.

"The Cowboy is another of my competitors." Sara realized Kirk and Logan hadn't seen the notes she'd made and given to Ryker earlier, and the men were having difficulty following Ryker's conversation. She explained as Ryker kept typing, probably sending this picture down to the police station, too. "The Cowboy's mother had a thing for the actor and named him after her movie idol. He and I had a business dinner a few months ago, and he suggested a merger."

Kirk practically growled at her. "What kind of merger?"

"My software, his hardware." She shoved her hair out of her eyes. "It wasn't personal, Kirk."

"Yeah, sure."

At the time, she hadn't thought the Cowboy had anything but business on his mind. But now that she thought back on that dinner, she realized she had missed his signals. The candles and wine she'd attributed to the restaurant's décor; the heat in the Cowboy's eyes, to his enthusiasm over his new digital photography enhancement system. But now she wondered if she could have been so wrapped up in her work and in Abby that she'd totally misconstrued his interest.

"If the Cowboy's in the Cayman Islands, he

couldn't have taken Abby from Gail at the bank,'' Sara reasoned.

''But he could have a partner,'' Kirk suggested.

''Other than money in the bank, have you found any connections between the dead man on the mountain and the Cowboy?'' Logan asked Ryker.

''I'm checking, boss.''

Logan picked up his phone again. This time he didn't leave the room, and she could plainly hear his end of the conversation.

''Sam? It's Logan Kincaid. Know where I can find a hardware expert at bargain prices?''

Sara realized that the kidnapper would want proof that her software worked. Giving him the hard drive wouldn't be enough. He'd want to run the program, and her computer was shot the moment she had torn out the wiring to spark the fire back on the mountain.

''Make it an hour and you have a deal,'' Logan told the man he'd called, then hung up. ''Sam's the best computer geek in Silicon Valley.''

Only Logan Kincaid would call Sam Brandson a computer geek. The industry icon owned a multinational conglomerate that spanned four continents. He was a genius and he also happened to have designed Sara's original hardware. That Logan had phoned him was no coincidence, and she marveled not just at Kincaid's knowledge but at his connections.

''You think Sam can modify a laptop to run my program in time to meet the kidnapper's demand.'' Sara's system wouldn't work with just any laptop. She needed extra processors, faster circuits, special integrated chips. Her equipment had been custom designed for her usage. Horrified that she might blow her one chance to get Abby back safely, she sagged with worry.

Web came up beside her. "With Sam's help, can you make the program work, then let me add a self-destruct mechanism?"

Sara shook her head. "These men are bright. Garth Davis graduated tops in his class at MIT. The Cowboy is a self-taught talent who heads a company that could rival Microsoft within ten years. Both of these men have exceptional mental skills. I won't take any chances with Abby's life."

Logan didn't say a word, and the room filled with silence. She supposed she'd insulted them without meaning to. "I'm sorry, but I don't want to risk my daughter's life on the chance that either of these men might detect a virus."

Kirk drew her aside into one of the bedrooms. "Sara, have a little trust in these men. They'll get Sara back. They know what they're doing."

Web, walking so quietly that she hadn't heard him follow them, spoke to her calmly. "I understand your concern. How about if you prepare two working computers, one with the self-destruct and one without it? Then you can decide later."

His suggestion sounded reasonable, but Sara wasn't backing down, even if she did appear to be casting aspersions on the abilities of the ex-CIA agent trying to help her. "Just because *you* can't recognize a tampered hard drive when you see one doesn't mean the kidnapper can't."

Web lowered his voice. "I shouldn't tell you this, and if you repeat what I'm about to mention, I'll deny

I ever said it—even in a court of law. Even if subpoenaed by Congress. But I've created a few viruses that even the KGB can't detect.''

The man wasn't boasting. In fact, his quiet, confident words reminded her of another man who knew his abilities to be superior but rarely spoke of them—her ex-husband. Sara recognized the same staunch belief in his expert skills in this man as she did in her husband.

Ex-husband, she reminded herself.

''Okay. We'll make two laptops, one with a virus, and decide later which one to use.''

''We've got another match,'' Ryker reported from the living room.

''You won't be disappointed,'' Web promised her.

Sara, Kirk and Web returned to the others. The pilot sat on the sofa next to Travis. Their heads together, they looked at a map. Logan peered at Ryker's computer screen.

''What's up?'' Kirk asked.

''Ely and the Cowboy both belonged to the same on-line guild.''

''Which guild?'' Logan asked.

''What's a guild?'' Kirk asked.

''A guild is a group of people who band together on the Internet to play other guilds,'' Sara explained to Kirk.

''They play Ever Quest.'' Ryker told them. ''It's popular. One of those role-playing—''

''I've heard of it,'' Logan said.

Web grinned at his boss. ''Logan, didn't you win the world playoffs under the code name Inferno, while trying to solve a murder for the—?''

"That's classified and we have guests," Logan reminded him.

Web's teasing flowed off his broad shoulders. Sara suspected not much would make Logan Kincaid uncomfortable—not even playing a game meant for juveniles.

Ryker must have been conversing with another guild member. "The Cowboy has a reputation for being the brains of the operation. Ely was the ruthless one."

"Just because they played an Internet game together doesn't make them kidnappers, either," Sara muttered. "Either Garth or the Cowboy could have Abby." She hoped Gail might identify one of the men to narrow the possibilities.

An hour later, security let Sam Brandson, the leader of one of Silicon Valley's largest hardware companies, through the door. Short, wearing a dove-gray five-thousand-dollar custom-made business suit and soft Italian leather shoes and carrying a paper-laden briefcase, he strode toward Logan and held out his hand.

"This better be good. I was in the middle of a lawsuit and my lawyers aren't happy with the delay, although I admit to feeling like a kid playing hooky." Sam grinned at Logan. "You must have some clout, for the judge to delay the trial and give me the afternoon off."

"Good to see you again, Sam." Logan shook his hand. "Would you mind if we got started right away? We don't have a lot of time."

"Sure." Sam slid his briefcase onto a table and pulled out two laptop computers and a bag of tools. "We just need to fill in the blanks."

Just then, the phone rang again.

Chapter Thirteen

At the sound of the phone, Kirk checked his watch, realizing eight hours had gone by since they'd last heard from the kidnapper. Abby had been taken from them this morning, and it was now dark outside. None of them had taken a break except to hit the bathroom. Travis and Logan had drunk cup after cup of coffee. Ryker had kept up his caffeine buzz with his sodas.

Sara had had to pump milk from her swollen breasts. Kirk knew she must be uncomfortable, and couldn't imagine how sad she must feel each time she performed that task.

Neither Kirk nor Sara had eaten a thing, but he wished he'd eaten a few crackers. Especially when Sara picked up the phone and the acid seemed to burn a hole through his stomach lining.

"Hello?"

"Can Billy come out and play?"

The voice on the speaker phone sounded like a kid's—definitely not the kidnapper.

Sara paled in confusion. "Who is this?"

"Sorry. I must have the wrong number."

Since they'd rerouted all the calls from the switchboard to come through directly, they also got wrong numbers. Kirk wished he could make her feel better or take some of her burden onto his own shoulders. He hating seeing the frantic worry in her eyes and realized he'd probably put that same look on her face every time he'd set out on a dangerous mission. Except that for him, she'd put on a brave front. He cursed himself for putting her through such trauma.

If she would only take him back, give them another chance, he'd never do this to her again. But first, they had to find Abby. His heart ached for the daughter he'd come to love in less a week. He couldn't imagine how much worse it was for Sara, who had carried the child in her womb, birthed her, breast-fed her and cared for her for the past nine months.

Sara sank back into the chair and rubbed her eyes. "I don't know how much more of this I can take."

Kirk wanted to sweep her into his arms and assure her that they would get Abby back. But Sara wouldn't accept false hope. She always faced problems head-on, and he'd always admired her courage for doing so.

"Hang in there." Ryker tried to give them some encouragement. "I'm checking every piece of property Garth owns. His credit card bills are interesting, too. For a married man, he travels from Michigan to Miami often. And he phones this house down there from his cell phone and never from his house phone."

"What does that tell us?" Sara asked, clearly trying to distract herself from the upsetting wrong number.

"The man's got a mistress," Logan guessed.

"Expensive dinners, flowers, jewelry. Oh yeah, he's cheating on his wife," Ryker confirmed.

"Do you have a phone number and address for his mistress?" Kirk asked.

"Sure." Ryker handed him a slip of paper.

Sara looked to Kirk with a mixture of agony and hope. He explained his theory as he dialed. "I'm betting that if Garth took the baby, he brought her to his mistress."

"Don't be direct," Logan warned.

"Not to worry." Kirk waited for the woman to answer.

On the fourth ring, she finally picked up the phone. "Yes?"

Kirk spoke in a bored tone, adding a touch of a southern accent. "I'm calling from Miami Carpet Service. Would you like your free cleaning tomorrow morning or afternoon, ma'am?"

"Carpet cleaning? You must be mistaken."

"Is your address 54821 Palm River Drive?"

"Yes."

"Well, you've won three rooms of free cleaning." Kirk hesitated. "Unless you want me to cancel?"

When he heard the distinct cry of a baby in the background, his hopes escalated but he tamped them down. The woman was silent, and Kirk put his hand over the mouthpiece.

Ryker's magic fingers searched through airline databases. "I'm finding clues on Garth's credit cards. Cross-checking with the airlines. I've found a plane ticket for Garth Davis from L.A. to Miami. Apparently he isn't using false ID."

"It's more difficult to get since September eleventh," Logan muttered.

"Thanks to the equipment we confiscated for the government last month," Jack Donovan added. "What's the ETA on the flight?"

"Arrived a couple of hours ago."

Garth's mistress finally responded, sounding flustered. "Come tomorrow morning."

Kirk hung up the phone. "I heard a baby crying."

"Can you book us on a flight to Miami?" Kirk asked Logan, already standing and eager to go after his child. As if sensing the urgency of the mission, Pepper also rose to her feet, her eyes alert.

Logan spoke to Ryker. "Contact the Air Force. The whole team's relocating to Florida."

Sam Brandson stood. "If you won't be needing my services, I'll head back to—"

"If you haven't yet completed the hardware modifications, I'm afraid you'll have to come with us," Logan gently told the man.

"But my trial?"

"I'll have the judge postpone."

"But—"

"Please." Sara stood, too, her eyes wide, her tone sincere. "We may need your help. They may not turn over our baby unless I can show them a working program."

Sam really had no choice, but he didn't realize it yet. From his side vision, Kirk saw that Web was closing in and clearly intended to use force if necessary. As if reading Web's mind, Jack Donovan's hand had gone to his weapon.

Travis, the negotiator, eased in, realizing force

wouldn't be necessary. "Thanks for agreeing to help us, sir. Our government is in your debt."

"Maybe we shouldn't leave," Sara said. "Suppose the kidnapper calls back with a place to bring the ransom?"

"I'll forward all calls to a special cell phone." Logan held up a spare phone and gave it to Sara. "For all practical purposes, the kidnapper will believe we're still here in California."

Thirty minutes later, Jack Donovan flew them out of California at supersonic speed.

BY MORNING LOGAN HAD LEASED a van, and a sign painter had worked through the night on triple time to paint on the side panel a professional advertisement in red and blue that read Miami Carpet Service.

Sara and Kirk had wanted to go to the house as soon as possible, but Logan had sent Web to watch the perimeter and had convinced them to wait until morning. He didn't want to go in, guns blazing, for fear of the baby's safety. Better to sneak in undercover.

At least they knew with some certainty that Garth was the kidnapper. From inside a holding cell at the Los Angeles police station, Gail had identified Garth Davis from a photo as the man who'd taken the baby from her outside the bank. The grandmother had cooperated fully with the District Attorney, and the DA believed she'd done so, not to wrangle a lighter sentence, but out of genuine concern for another child. The DA had also passed on the news that Gail's granddaughter had had the bone-marrow transplant and was doing as well as could be expected.

Although Sara and Sam had spent half the night preparing the drive to work with her program and she was exhausted, she still couldn't relax. Jack and Travis had spelled Web at Garth's house, saying they'd seen his mistress—who they now knew to be Rita Hernandez—through the windows several times, but not the baby or Garth.

In the end, Sara decided that Web's alterations were undetectable and told him they could go with the machine with the programmed virus—which would self-destruct on the second run. After spending the past twenty-four hours with these men, Sara trusted their judgment more than she had earlier, and she didn't want Garth to steal her work and then sell it to a terrorist organization.

She and Kirk had spent the rest of the night together, not talking, but she'd taken comfort from his presence. Being alone would have been intolerable. And when he'd embraced her, she'd accepted his comfort in the manner in which it was given, freely, no strings attached.

Before the team had departed for a few hours of sleep, Sara had insisted on riding in the van with the men the next day. Logan hadn't argued, which pleased her. She'd assured him that she would stay out of the way, but needed to be there when they rescued Abby.

Perhaps the lack of energy was as much physical as mental. Although she wasn't pumping as much milk as Abby usually ate, her milk hadn't dried up and the painful process had taken a toll. Or perhaps she hadn't yet fully recovered from the ordeal on the mountain. But this past week had changed them all.

Although at nine months of age Abby could now drink from a cup, and Sara had intended to switch her to baby food soon, Sara resented that Garth and his greed had taken the decision out of her hands.

More than anything in the world, Sara wanted Abby back. Her heart almost broke every time she thought of all the things that could go wrong. Garth might not give up the baby easily. And the thought preyed on her mind that none of the observers on Logan's team had spotted Garth or the baby.

And things between Kirk and her remained unresolved. When she had booted him out, he'd gone too easily. Kirk was stubborn and she'd been sure he would try to win her back. That he would come to her side when she and Abby needed him, without hesitation, without any I-told-you-so's, only proved that he may have lost a battle, but fully intended to win the campaign.

Finally morning arrived.

Garth's mistress, Rita Hernandez, was expecting to have her carpets cleaned this morning. But would she let them through the locked gate? Sara sat tensely beside Kirk on the back bench of the van carrying the name Miami Carpet Services. Logan drove the van; Travis took over the front passenger seat. Web and Jack were hidden on the grounds, and Sam had flown back to California.

The neighborhood of sprawling homes on the intracoastal waterway was inhabited by the rich and famous. Huge royal palm trees stood like sentries outside elaborate fences and gatehouses. All the mansions in the area seemed to have locked gates and security cameras.

Logan checked his weapon, keeping the gun below the dash and out of sight before reholstering it at his ankle. The man appeared as natural in his crinkled white uniform as he did in his expensive suits. He may have looked like a man from the carpet service, but his tone conveyed authority.

"Everyone keep your heads up. By now, Rita may have spoken to Garth and warned him about the free carpet cleaning."

While a stationary, remote camera focused on the van, Logan pulled up to the gate and pressed a button next to a speaker. "Miami Carpet."

Would the woman let them inside? Beside Sara, Kirk twined his fingers through hers, just as tense as she was. Sara held her breath, one hand in Kirk's, the other rubbing the cell phone.

A SERVANT BUZZED THEM through the front gate and instructed Logan to enter through the side door. Apparently the front entrance was reserved for guests and family.

Logan parked, and Sara and Kirk stayed in the van. Logan exited the vehicle and entered the house with paperwork on a clipboard. Travis opened the back of the van and unloaded a machine.

She couldn't see Web or Jack, but she knew they were somewhere on the grounds, watching the premises. With the air-conditioning off and the windows open, the van quickly grew warm as the minutes ticked by.

For the next half hour Kirk and Sara waited in the warm vehicle and drank bottled water. She could barely swallow but forced the water down. Sara tried not to think how she would react if Logan didn't come out of that house with Abby cradled in his arms. She tried not to think about the future. Tried not to think at all.

Finally Logan returned to the van. His arms empty. No baby in sight.

Sara started to shake. Logan slid behind the wheel, and Web and Jack appeared from the tropical shrubbery and took the middle seats. The men's faces were grim, yet expectant.

"She wasn't there?" Abby asked.

"Garth got suspicious about the phone call about our free carpet cleaning," Logan explained as he drove out the front gate. "Rita says he disappeared with the baby last night within ten minutes of our call."

Kirk frowned and held Sara tightly. "Rita cooperated?"

"She was suspicious of Garth showing up with a baby and a wild story that didn't make sense. She wanted no part of his scheme. When I pointed out that she could be seen as a co-conspirator because she didn't call the police, she became very cooperative."

Sara spoke through a mouth dry with tension despite all the water she'd sipped. The air conditioner hummed but would take a while to cool down the vehicle. "Did she say where he took Abby?"

"She doesn't know." Logan shrugged. "Rita could be lying, but I believed her. She gave information freely and intended to pack her clothes and vacate the premises. Even gave us her parents' address, where she intends to stay for a while."

Oh God.

The man had fled with her child. He'd had twelve hours head start and could have left the country by now. Sara's panic started to escalate, but as if reading her thoughts, Kirk twisted in the seat beside her, cupped her chin and forced her to look into his serious eyes.

"Garth knows that he'll never get your software unless he takes care of Abby."

Sara held onto the thought and glanced down at the laptop stuffed into a satchel by her feet. During the flight to Florida she'd copied the program onto a spare computer, then Web had given her drive a virus. The system, called Carnivore, would eat itself within either an hour after anyone opened it or upon a second run. And Web had added a fail-safe device inside so Garth couldn't make copies before the program cannibalized itself.

But the plan to foil her enemy gave her no comfort. Her work paled into insignificance compared to Abby. Would she ever see their child again?

She glanced at the cell phone and prayed for it to ring.

Logan looked at her in his rearview mirror. "Rita told me that she fed and bathed Abby last night. He's taking care of her, Sara."

While they spoke, Ryker had opened his computer and was perusing his research. "Garth owns a hunting lodge in the swamps an hour east of here. He keeps a luxury sailboat docked at the marina and a penthouse condominium in the city."

"The marina is close. Why don't we swing by and check it out," Travis suggested.

Logan pulled over to the curb and handed Jack a

cardboard tube. "I brought a peel-and-stick sign. Place this over the painted carpet cleaning advertisement."

Several minutes later, Jack rejoined the others in the van. "We're now officially a sightseeing group."

They'd been riding toward the marina for several minutes in silence, except for Ryker typing away, when Sara's cell phone rang.

She automatically looked to Travis for last-minute instructions. He didn't fail her. "Remember that you're supposed to be in California. If he's in Florida and wants to meet, buy us extra time to get here."

Sara didn't want to buy time. She wanted to speed up the process. She wanted Abby back, and the sooner the better. But she understood the necessity of planning the ransom payoff carefully, so she'd try to do as Travis suggested.

Don't blow it. Keep him talking. Stall. Ask to speak to Abby. Don't let him know that we know his identity.

Ryker had assured her the cell phone call could still be traced—if they stayed on the line long enough. She'd drilled the rules into her memory for hours, but she stilled feared making a mistake that could cost dearly. For Kirk, who had no role to play but who had to sit by her side and watch, the inactivity was just as bad, if not worse. She could read his concern by the lack of expression on his face, the way he sat so still.

Sara pressed the phone's green button. "Hello?"

"Have you got the hardware and software up and running?" The same mechanized voice reverberated from the speaker.

"I want to talk to Abby. And turn off the damn

mechanized voice. I need to hear *her* voice.'' Sara spoke firmly and calmly. Travis had also explained to her that the more upset she sounded, the less likely Garth would be to grant her wishes. And she dearly wanted to hear Abby coo into the phone.

Garth ignored her question. ''The program?''

''The baby?'' Sara could be just as curt, just as demanding. She really didn't expect Garth to put the baby on the phone, so when he muttered, ''I don't think she'll talk, but I'll put the phone to her ear. Just a second. Talk.''

''Abby, darling. It's Mama. Talk to me, baby. Say Mama. Please, honey, say Mama.''

''Ma-ma-ma-ma. Mama.''

At the sound of Abby's baby voice, Sara had to blink back tears. Her heart swelled with hope and she could see a suspicious gleam of moisture in Kirk's eyes, as well.

''Enough of the baby talk,'' the mechanized voice came back. ''Tell me about the program.''

Sara gulped. This is where she could stall. ''I didn't want to risk storing the program on the Web. I figured you'd want the one and only copy. And even a CD-ROM doesn't have enough space, the program is too big.''

''Hurry up.''

''I placed the program on a specialized laptop hard drive. I'll bring the equipment, and you can test it.''

''Good. Give these coordinates to your friends.'' He gave sets of numbers that she assumed were latitude and longitude. ''Helicopter in. Come alone and unarmed. Have the chopper fly back to the city.

Bring your phone and your walking shoes. You've got one hour.''

Ryker turned around and whispered to her, "The meet is in the Florida swamp."

While she talked, Logan used his own phone to begin making arrangements.

She was supposed to be in California. Sara thought quickly. "It'll take me a half hour to get to the airport. Four to five hours to fly to the other coast, and then—"

"Cut the crap," Garth ordered. "That bitch Rita may have betrayed me, but my servants know which side their bread is buttered on."

Sara realized that someone in the house could have overheard Rita's conversation with Logan and reported it to Garth. Or possibly just the van showing up in the driveway had alerted a watcher to their presence. Either way, they'd had no choice but to take that risk, especially while they were still hoping Abby might be in the mansion.

Ryker held up both hands. If she could keep Garth on the line ten more seconds, he could trace the call.

Sara tried, sweat dripping down her brow despite the van's air-conditioning system. "It's not that easy. I've got to lease a helicopter and a pilot."

"One hour or—" The line went dead. She looked at Ryker.

"We narrowed his location down to Florida, but we already knew that."

Chapter Fourteen

Exactly one hour later, Sara climbed out of the helicopter at the coordinates Garth had given her. She held the hard drive and documentation in a bag slung over her shoulder. As she looked through the cypress trees, she hoped she could keep all of her instructions straight.

Logan had her outfitted in a long-sleeved shirt, long slacks that tucked into knee-high boots and a hat with mosquito netting to protect her face. She carried enough gear to make her ten pounds heavier, and her boots sank into the squishy loam.

Logan had refused to arm her with a weapon, claiming that she needed to follow Garth's instructions exactly, but Kirk had slipped her a revolver, which she'd tucked into her pocket. She more than appreciated that Kirk trusted her skill with the weapon and, more importantly, her judgment. Hopefully Garth wouldn't pat her down and would assume she'd followed his instructions. She felt better with the weapon heavy in her pocket. This swamp was wild enough for her to meet up with a snake or an alligator, but she feared the two-legged adversary the most.

However, she no longer shook. Glad to be doing something, she shoved all her fears aside, grateful that she could function. In fact, she seemed to be especially clearheaded.

While she was supposed to do exactly as Garth commanded, she would make decisions as she went along. Logan had rigged her cell phone so that he could monitor all her calls, listening in to any conversation if Garth phoned her again. Then she had a second phone to call the team if she had questions or needed help. But they would not call her and suggested she not call them unless absolutely necessary, in case Garth was monitoring her actions from close by.

She had water in her canteen, a compass and a GPS that Kirk had shown her how to use. In a knapsack she lugged bug spray, power bars, a first aid kit, baby formula, diapers, flares, a mirror and a baby sling. Most important was the scent she carried on the soles of her boots and around her ankles. Kirk had sprayed her with a substance that she couldn't smell, but which would leave traces on the ground, allowing Pepper to track her if the electronics failed. One thing she'd noticed about Logan Kincaid that reassured her: the man always had a backup plan for his backup plans. But what gave her even more confidence was that Kirk was out there. No one was better than he was at tracking. No one else cared more. And no one was as determined to succeed.

The plan was simple. Sara was to wait until Garth contacted her and then do whatever he said. Slowly. Her goal, to delay him, would allow Kirk and Web to catch up to her. They'd taken an airboat into the swamp and would hike to meet her. Since they could only motor within five miles of her position without giving away their location by the sound of their engines, she had to delay Garth long enough for them to reach her. However, Kirk and Web planned to remain hidden until she had Abby back in her arms or until the last possible moment that she still had a chance to get her baby back.

So far, she'd been on the ground five minutes and the last hum of the chopper's rotors was long gone. She hadn't seen anything resembling a man or machine. However, frogs croaked and whooping cranes perched in the trees. She was grateful for the waterproof boots she wore as she spied tiny bubbles in the mushy ground under her feet.

Sara checked her watch. Logan had told her that it could take the men as much as an hour to reach her. As she looked around, she realized his estimate might have been optimistic. Canals wound their way between clumps of high grasses and marsh, making walking in a straight line impossible. The hot, dank air filled with the smell of rotting logs made her long for the crisp air of the Rocky Mountains. There, at least, they'd all been together, and she couldn't help wondering if they would ever be together again.

Even though she knew that every precious second of delay was good, the nerve-racking wait made her uneasy. A turtle sunning itself on a log plopped into the water, drawing her attention to the surrounding area. Was Garth hiding behind the next clump of bushes, waiting to attack? He could steal the legal documents and hard drive, then shoot her, believing he could get away with murder. She told herself he would want to verify that the program worked before he attempted to kill her, and a test would take some time. He'd already made the mistake of assuming he had the program once, after he'd crashed her plane on the mountain. He wouldn't make that mistake again.

When her cell phone rang, she waited the requisite two rings before answering. "Yes?"

"Turn around," the mechanized voice commanded.

He must be close enough to be watching her. Despite the sunny Florida heat, a chill scampered down her spine.

If Garth could see her, she might be able to spot him with the binoculars, but she didn't dare search. Instead, she did as directed and turned, slowly, deliberately stopping at 160 degrees instead of a complete 180. "Okay?"

"Keep turning."

She overturned, winced at the curse in her ear and then fortified herself with the notion that she wanted him to believe her a complete klutz while away from her computer.

"Look up."

"What am I looking for?" she asked.

And then she saw a light puff of smoke that dissipated all too quickly. Immediately she recognized the brilliance of his plan. He hadn't steered her by voice over the phone or even issued coordinates for her GPS. Unless someone stood in her exact line of sight, they wouldn't be able to spot his signal very easily, if at all. And the place he'd indicated, an island surrounded by a large body of water, would allow him to see if anyone followed.

Damn. Damn. Damn.

"Did you see my signal?"

She wanted to say no, to stall, but didn't quite dare. Garth might have stood in her exact spot to gauge whether she would have a clear view of the signal. And if she lied and he caught her lying, he could take out his anger on the baby.

"Yeah, I see it." So she came up with another way to stall. "I might be able to get there from here, but I can't walk on water."

"Listen to me very carefully. Your baby's life depends on your obeying me *exactly*."

At his threat, ice coated her veins, making her hands and feet go numb. Sara had never concentrated so hard in her entire life.

"Look behind the bushes to your right and don't say a word except to tell me that you've found the object hidden there."

Sara walked to the bushes and peered through the thicket. A canoe with a paddle awaited her. She'd always known Garth had a brilliant mind but she hadn't known he could be so devious.

Once she got inside that boat, Pepper would lose her scent and it would be almost impossible for Kirk and Web to approach the island without being seen. And she didn't trust the tracking device that Logan had inserted into her long-sleeved shirt to work if the canoe tipped and she got wet. She wanted to leave a more physical type of marker for Kirk and Web to follow, but had to be careful. Garth was probably still watching her.

Sara strode to the side of the canoe. She started to push the boat into the water and deliberately rocked it. She fell onto her butt. While she was down, she quickly drew an arrow sign in the mud with her finger, hiding the action with her body as much as possible.

Then she stood, shoved the canoe into the water and paddled toward where she'd seen the smoke. She paddled awkwardly, slowly and took frequent rests, even lifting the canteen to her lips and pretending to drink when she didn't yet need fluids. She had to stall for time and pray that Kirk would somehow catch up with her. And if he didn't, she had to find a way to save Abby.

KIRK HADN'T BEEN PLEASED when Logan insisted that Web accompany him. But he hadn't argued, knowing that a discussion would waste precious time. He just decided he wouldn't slow down, and if Web fell behind, that would be his problem.

But Web kept up the harsh pace with a resilience that told Kirk the man was in excellent shape. They were jogging through a marsh with soggy footing, with packs on their backs that weighed upwards of forty pounds. Sweat poured from their bodies, and they drank from their canteens on the run to replace body fluids. The only time they stopped was when Kirk gave Pepper water.

While the dog drank, Web pulled out the electronic tracker. He stared at the scope and frowned. "We've got a problem."

"What?"

"Garth's jamming our signals on all frequencies."

Sara had told them Garth was smart. Garth had understood right from the beginning that Sara had help from experts and he'd countered with his own expertise. But Garth wouldn't be counting on a dog finding him—at least, Kirk hoped not.

''Pepper works on scent and should hone in on Sara once we close within one mile.''

Since the equipment no longer worked, Web ditched it. There was no point in carrying any more weight than necessary.

Pepper finished her water and they moved out, Pepper leading the way, followed by Kirk, with Web bringing up the rear. Kirk and Pepper couldn't run at this crushing pace all day. Not in this heat. Not packing this kind of weight. Kirk was counting on catching up to Sara as soon as possible.

As they closed in on her, they would have to modify their pace and search for cover, which would slow them even more. They'd have to stay out of sight and remain extremely quiet to avoid detection. But first they had to get there.

When Web took out a phone and listened to Sara conversing with the enemy, Kirk had to refrain from yanking the phone from the other man's hands. Not that this would have been an easy task. Web moved with the ease of a highly trained athlete, and he possessed those calloused ridges on his hands that told Kirk he had other skills. Deadly skills. Kirk was glad the man was on their side.

Web rewarded his patience with information. ''Garth just gave her directions to a new location.''

''Where?''

''He didn't say, just sent a smoke signal, instead.''

''Good. Pepper will smell the smoke, won't you, girl?''

Fear for Sara and Abby had Kirk pushing the dog and Web and himself at an exhausting pace. He put out of his mind the possibility of running into an ambush, hoping that Garth would work alone. He tried not to think how easily they could be picked off by a sniper, despite their camouflage gear. He put out of his mind how out of her element Sara was right now. She'd done fine in the blizzard; she'd cope with the swamp.

His main concern was that if they couldn't catch up, Sara might end up facing Garth alone. That's why he'd given her the gun. No doubt Garth thought Sara a computer nerd, which she could use to her advantage.

Well, she might be a brilliant programmer, but she was so much more. She was a great mother to Abby. And she'd been a good wife to him.

She was honest and loyal and everything Kirk wanted in a woman. Best of all, she was adaptable. She could think outside the box. And boy, could she think. What other woman could start a fire with a computer and a diaper?

But now she was walking into danger, risking her life to save her child's, willing to give up ten years of work and millions of dollars without a second thought in order to rescue their baby. And she needed his help. He *had* to get there. Soon.

Pepper whined low in her throat, signaling that the scent might be coming to an end. With all the water surrounding them, Kirk wasn't surprised. Still, as both men stopped behind Pepper and stared at the water, Kirk's heart sank.

Pepper closed in on some bushes, and Kirk read the tracks carefully. A narrow boat had crushed the plants. Sara's footprint indicated that she'd been here alone. Kirk smiled when he saw her arrow drawn in the mud, but his grin quickly disappeared as he realized she'd headed to the island.

Web hauled him back into the trees. "I have an inflatable boat in my pack, big enough for two men and a dog, but we can't help Sara if we're shot on the way over."

"We could swim, but Garth would still spot us."

"Not if we swim underwater."

Kirk shook his head. "It'll take at least ten minutes to swim that far. I don't know about you, but I can't hold my breath that long. Maybe we could find some reeds to breathe through."

Logan had outfitted this mission. "I have two rebreathers and swim goggles in my pack," said Web.

Kirk had never used SEAL equipment, but he saw the advantage immediately. A rebreather was a small device that fit into the mouth and drew oxygen out of the water, allowing the men to stay hidden under the surface. The problem was Pepper. Not even Logan could equip the dog to swim completely under the surface.

"You take care of sorting the gear, I'll fix up a camouflage for Pepper." Kirk dumped his pack beside Web, trusting the man's judgment of what to take with them and what to leave behind. Too much weight would slow them down, yet they wanted to remain prepared when they reached the island.

In the meantime, Kirk quickly found a thick branch with massive leaves and more branches fanning out the top. Using an ax and his knife, he carved the wood, holding it up to Pepper's shoulders, whittling it until the branch rested comfortably against her chest.

Lashing the rope around the branch, he attached his creation to the patient dog. Not the least bit afraid, only curious, Pepper stood still, trusting him completely.

"We're going for a swim, girl."

Kirk tested his invention out of sight of the island. Pepper could swim completely hidden by the cover of log and branches. Although the drag slowed her, the natural flotation of the wood didn't pull her down.

However, he couldn't say the same for his boots, which filled with water and weighed far too much for him to wear while swimming. Web, wearing nothing by skivvies, met him on the bank as Kirk was removing his boots, his shirt and slacks. In the water, he'd wear boxers and a pack that now contained the bare essentials—a knife, a gun and matches in a dry bag, and a compass.

Web surveyed Pepper's camouflage. "Is she okay with that?"

"Dogs like Pepper are trained to accept all kinds of unusual situations. While I don't need to stay by her side during our swim, I'd prefer to be there to remove the branch after we reach the island."

Web eyed him. "Think you can make it there alone?"

"Sure. Why?"

"We've got a major problem."

Kirk hadn't spent much time with Web, but the man wasn't prone to talking, much less to exaggerating. When he said they had a major problem, Kirk's pulse sped up.

"What's up?"

"I scouted what I could of the island with high-powered binoculars. I didn't see Sara or her canoe. But I did spy an airboat for Garth to make a quick getaway. I need to prevent his escape. You go after Sara."

"Got it." Kirk accepted the rebreather and stepped into the water beside Pepper. He pointed to the island and spoke to her. "We go there." After he was sure Pepper understood, he ducked under the surface, appreciating the cool temperature and glad he could rely on the dog's sense of direction.

The water was dark, and even through his goggles he saw nothing but blackness.

SARA PULLED THE CANOE onto the island's bank. She longed to turn around and search for Kirk, but didn't give in to the weakness. The last thing she wanted to do was alert Garth that Kirk and Web were on the way. Remembering to stall for every precious second, she lifted the canteen to her lips and allowed the water to cool her parched throat.

Carefully and deliberately she screwed the cap back on, then reattached the canteen to her belt. Now what?

Garth hadn't given her any further directions since the one telephone call. Surveying the bank, she realized that this cleared area was pretty much the only spot on which she could have landed. So if Garth had left her any kind of message it should be in sight. But she saw nothing. No note tacked to a tree. No notebook propped up on a pile of logs.

"Place the satchel with the documents and the program on the ground by your feet."

When Garth called out to her from a hidden location, she jumped. But the program and rights of ownership were the only bargaining chip she had to get Abby back. Sara didn't move, except to raise her chin and straighten her spine.

"I want to see my daughter."

Garth fired a shot at Sara's feet. "You are in no position to bargain."

Sara ignored the bullet, braced her feet wider and bluffed, stalling for time. "I have no reason to give you the documents if you cannot produce my child."

"I should just shoot you."

"But you won't. Not until you see the program run," she called out, turning slightly so she could scan the water behind her with a sideways glance. She saw no boat, no bubbles—only a clump of grasses floating her way. "I won't enter the password to turn on the system unless you bring me my daughter."

"You could always make another baby, Sara."

"I'm partial to this one." She had to stay strong and pay attention. She didn't want to give Garth any cause to flee or to harm her or the baby. She swung the satchel off her shoulder and let the strap rest in her hand. "You want my program. Well, here it is. Bring me my child and let's get this over with. I don't like swamps and mosquitoes. I much prefer my nice clean office with screens and air-conditioning."

Keep talking. Distract him.

Not for one moment did she want him to notice that the suspicious clump of grasses was floating toward them much too rapidly.

"You know, Garth, if I'd known you wanted my work so badly, I would have considered selling it to you."

Finally, she spied the man dropping to his feet from his perch in a tree. He strode toward her, a rifle resting in the crook of his arm.

There was no sign of Abby, and despair chilled her heart.

Chapter Fifteen

Kirk pulled himself onto the bank, making as little noise as possible. The swim had taken longer than he'd anticipated, since he'd had to change his direction after he spied Garth in the clearing with Sara. There was no sign of Abby.

Kirk unhooked Pepper from the branches lashed to her. She immediately shook off the water droplets, but Garth was shouting so loudly he didn't seem to notice.

Kirk took out an article of clothing Abby had recently worn and thrust it toward Pepper's nose. She sniffed and her ears perked up. "Find Abby, girl."

From the clearing, Garth's tone rose in volume. "Don't play me for a fool, woman."

"Would you please calm down." Sara sounded like the voice of reason, but somewhat stressed out. "You're making me nervous. When I get nervous, I make mistakes."

Kirk took out his weapon and headed straight toward the woman he loved and the man threatening his family. After the long helicopter ride, a run through the woods and his swim, he was finally close enough to see Sara. She was sitting on the ground with the laptop, concentrating on her typing. Garth aimed the rifle at her head.

Kirk wouldn't have hesitated to shoot the man if he knew the baby's location. He kept hoping that Garth would live up to his end of the bargain, but Kirk had a bad feeling in his gut. And Sara had told him that if he could only save her or the baby, he was to save Abby.

What a horrible choice to make. Although he'd agreed to her demand to make her happy, Kirk prayed he never had to make that kind of agonizing decision. He intended to go home with both of his girls.

With Sara between Kirk and Garth, her back to him, he had difficulty seeing exactly what she was doing. However, there could be no mistaking when Sara handed the laptop to Garth.

"You've got what you wanted—now where is my child?"

Garth motioned to her satchel with his gun. "What's the password?"

Her back still to Kirk, she told him. "It'll take two minutes to process and open."

Garth stared at the screen, waiting. Kirk held very still, unwilling to alert Garth to his presence. He kept hoping Sara would convince the man to tell her where he was keeping their daughter.

"Aren't you going to test the program?" Sara asked.

In the distance, Pepper barked once sharply. From the sound of her bark, she'd found Abby's scent.

"You wouldn't have tried to trick me with your

daughter's life on the line.'' Garth cocked the gun and pointed the weapon straight at Sara.

From the bushes, Kirk took the only shot Garth offered. A head shot. Both men fired. Sara screamed but appeared to be okay.

Garth dropped his weapon. Apparently Kirk had gotten off his shot just soon enough to throw off the other man's aim. A crease of blood streaked from Garth's forehead and into his eyes, and he staggered backward, then spun around and ran.

Sara jumped to her feet and placed herself between Kirk's gun and Garth's back. ''Don't shoot him! He never told me where to find Abby.''

''Pepper's found her scent.''

Within thirty seconds, they heard the boat's motor roaring to life. Apparently Web hadn't had enough time to swim and disengage the engines.

Kirk took Sara's hand, and together they followed the sound of Pepper's excited barks.

Sara's voice rose with anxiety. ''I'm almost afraid to find her. What if he kill—''

''Abby's alive. I can tell from Pepper's barks.''

''I hope you're right.''

''Have a little faith in me, Sara.''

In front of them, the bushes parted and Web stepped from between the branches, holding a baby in his arms. *Abby!* An obviously excited and proud Pepper walked beside him.

Sara released Kirk's hand and broke into a run. ''Abby? Are you okay, sweetie?''

''That dog led me right to her. Garth had left her on the side bank wrapped in a blanket.'' Web grinned, and Kirk refrained from thinking about alligators.

"I'm no doctor but other than a few mosquito bites on her arms, she seems just fine."

The sound of the fleeing boat's motor suddenly died. As Sara held Abby to her chest in delight, tears of joy brimming from her eyes, Kirk glanced over her head at Web for an explanation.

"His boat just sprang a leak. He won't get far. The team will pick him up shortly."

"Abby. Abby. Abby. You had your mama so worried."

Her daddy, too. Kirk did not want to lose either of them again. Ever.

Abby looked from Sara to Kirk and broke into a huge smile. "Mama. Dada."

"That's right." His heart welled with love and pride. "You're back where you belong."

Epilogue

Two weeks later

Sara had felt it only fair to visit Kirk's ranch. After all, he'd remained with her until the government had purchased her software. Once again, with her daughter back in her arms, she had felt safe. Logan's team had successfully caught the fleeing Garth, and police had picked up the pilot who had crashed her plane. Both men would remain behind bars for a long time. For his part, the Cowboy appeared innocent of any wrongdoing. He had been on a charter fishing boat in the Cayman Islands for the past two weeks—simply on vacation.

She liked the peacefulness of the acreage Kirk had purchased outright with the cash Logan Kincaid had insisted on paying him for the mission. Even better, she liked the ramifications of his setting down permanent roots. In her mind, owning property meant permanency. She sat on the front porch, breathing in the crisp, clean air, and watched Abby squeal with pleasure as she hung onto Pepper to take her first wobbly steps. If only Sara could be sure Kirk's enthusiasm for the ranch would last, she'd take him back in a New York minute.

He thrived out here, and she adored having him to herself after having shared him with the U.S. Marine Corps for so many years. But she'd already seen a sign of the old restlessness in him. When Logan Kincaid had asked him for an answer about joining the Shey Group, Kirk had left the possibilities open, unwilling to commit himself but promising to take a look at future projects on a case-by-case basis.

Kirk took a seat beside her and placed a puppy in her lap. The dog wagged his tail and sniffed inquisitively.

Sara scratched the soft fur behind the floppy ears. "Abby's going to be walking soon."

"If you stay, I'll find time to add a spare bedroom onto the back—"

"*If* I stay, I'm building my dream house."

Kirk chuckled. "I like the idea of you spoiling me."

"I'm scared, Kirk."

He slipped his hand inside hers. "I know."

She had to be romantically challenged to question this man as her lifetime partner. He'd risked his life to save her and Abby, whom he obviously adored. "Suppose you got offered your dream job tomorrow?"

"That's not going to happen."

His firmness made her turn her head. His eyes, so fierce, so determinedly amused, so loving, never failed to burn straight to her heart. She loved Kirk, always had, always would. And she knew him well enough to tell when he kept secrets from her.

"What haven't you told me?"

"Last week, the Marines offered me command of their worldwide canine operations."

Her heart tripped and almost dropped to her stomach. "And?"

"I turned them down."

He'd turned them down. "For me? Suppose I don't change my mind about us getting back together? Won't you regret that decision?"

"Nope. I'm not leaving because I want to be near you so that I can change your mind. And if you choose to keep me at a distance, I'll still want to be near our daughter."

Sara could barely take in the magnitude of his revelation. He wasn't turning down his fantasy job because she'd asked it of him—but because he wanted to remain close. "What about Logan's offer?"

"Not all his missions are dangerous. Sometimes they do search and rescue. I've told him I'd give him an answer on a case-by-case basis. You'd be in on those decisions, okay?"

"You aren't going to change your mind, are you?"

"Nope."

With a gladness that made her forget the puppy in her lap, she looped her arms around his neck and tugged his head down for a kiss. "Marry me again, Kirk Hardaker."

The puppy leaped off her lap and headed toward Pepper and Abby to check out the fun.

At her bold proposal, amusement and love shimmered in Kirk's eyes. "I was wondering how long it would take for you to ask."

* * * * *

For a sneak at Susan Kearney's next book in the Heroes Inc. *series,*

GUARDING THE HEIRESS,

to be published in May 2003, turn the page...

Chapter One

Ryker Stevens blinked as a knock interrupted his latest attempt to integrate an unbreakable encryption program with his operating system. The techies down at Langley had come up with an awesome JavaScript, but installing the bugger had him bummed after he'd crashed his computer for the third time. Now nothing worked.

The door of his office opened. As Ryker took in his visitor, he lost all interest in his computer for the first time in several weeks. How could he think about software with the achy-breaky-heart hardware coming in his direction?

A high-maintenance woman like this one had never graced Ryker Steven's office before, and he could barely hold back an appreciative whistle. She didn't just walk, she strode toward him with a sexy sway of hips encased in a flowing black ankle-length skirt that ended at leather boots. Her soft tailored blouse swelled and nipped in at just the right places. He raised his eyes to her face, and she attempted a tentative smile of greeting, which failed.

This woman didn't need to smile to look good. She

didn't need the designer clothes she wore to draw attention to that killer body or the expertly applied makeup to improve her skin. Lordy, she was perfect, hot, except for the dark circles under her eyes that her makeup couldn't quite hide. She was the kind of woman a man fantasized about after he fell asleep surfing the Net, then woke up to find it'd all been a dream. Women like her came from uptown, the other side of the tracks, and they rarely sized him up with burdened hazel eyes that told him trouble weighed on them like a five-hundred-pound monster.

"Are you Ryker Stevens?" She spoke in a voice rough and low, as if she'd spent too many hours in long conversations or smoke-filled rooms.

"That depends on who wants to know." Ryker had been in tough spots quite a few times in his thirty years, and he immediately recognized the combination of hope and desperation on her expressive face.

"Let's not play games." The stranger opened her purse, took out a gold pen and a checkbook in elegant gilded leather. She scrawled her name across the signature spot, ripped the check free and shoved it across his desk—leaving him to fill in his name and the dollar amount. He wondered if the lady was usually into grand gestures, because she didn't seem the type. Despite her display of boldness, she was classy, refined, understated.

He read the name printed across the top of the check—Daria Harrington—then ignored the payment, making no move to touch the check. But suddenly Ryker's prodigious memory and ability to sort through seemingly stray facts kicked in. An old acquaintance of his, Harry Levine, had married a Harrington. If this woman was Harry's wife, his old friend had married not only money and class but beauty, too. Harry had invited him to the wedding, but he'd received the invitation months too late after returning from a mission in Saudi Arabia. Some guys had all the luck—even if their wives didn't take their names after the wedding ceremony.

"You're Harry's wife?"

"Sister-in-law," she corrected him, and before he could decide how he felt about that news, she threw him a zinger. "Harry's dead. I killed him."

Ryker would have laughed at the impossibility of the statement, except that, at the admission, her back straightened and her face paled. She tipped her chin up but her lower lip quivered.

"Was it an accident?" he asked.

"I murdered him."

She couldn't have shocked him more if she'd claimed to be from Mars.

Harry Levine, one of the CIA's top operatives, dead? Killed by *her*—after some of the most highly trained and skilled agents in the world had tried and failed?

Ryker cursed himself for holing up in his office to work steadily since he'd returned from Zaire, instead of paying attention to the news. He'd been living on pizza and Chinese for weeks. Since his office was the front room of his apartment, he could delve into a problem for as long as he wanted without leaving his place. Running a hand through his ragged hair, he tried to recall exactly how long it had been since he'd read a newspaper, watched television or even called up a headline on the Internet. Maybe several weeks.

No wonder he hadn't heard about Harry's death, which had to have made the papers since he'd married into such a prominent family.

He stared at Daria. From her chin-length chestnut hair down to her expensive boots, she looked like a socialite, like she belonged in the pages of a fashion magazine. Her eyes held his, but he sensed the effort it took. He saw determination, but not the eyes of a killer. Besides, wealthy daughters of prominent citizens usually didn't commit murder and then openly admit it. Yet Daria Harrington would hardly have come here claiming to be a murderer if she didn't believe her statement. Unless she was crazy.

She didn't look crazy. She looked worried.

And her brother-in-law had pulled Ryker's ass out of the fire once in Beijing and again in Panama. If not for Harry's impeccable timing and bravery, Ryker might still be rotting in a foreign prison. So he owed Harry, and even if Ryker did come from poor white trash, he always paid his debts.

That he had minutes ago been fantasizing over Harry's murderer disgusted him. And angered him. His voice was colder than he'd intended. "Please have a seat, Ms. Harrington."

"Where?" She looked at the only other chair in the room. It was filled with old circuit boards, a mouse, a broken motherboard, an Ethernet card and several empty pizza boxes.

He leaned over his desk, tilted the chair, ignored the crash as the equipment and trash topped onto the floor, then righted the chair. He supposed he should have stood and offered her a seat right off, maybe a drink to put her at ease. But what did he care about putting Harry's murderer at ease?

He still didn't completely believe she'd killed Harry, and he intended to get the entire story from her—especially why she wanted to hire him. If what she said was true, if she'd killed Harry, he was the last person to come to for help.

Had her rich father with his connections galore suggested she hire the services of the Shey Group? But money wasn't enough to hire the team Ryker worked with. They only accepted the cases of the good guys. The Shey Group wasn't just pricey, they were picky.

As a covert team of men with top-secret government clearances, the Shey Group took on dangerous and seemingly impossible missions. They had the luxury of turning down more assignments than they accepted—despite the very hefty fees they charged.

Ryker loved the interesting nature of his work. Top-secret clearances meant using the latest technological wizardry. And their boss's, Logan Kincaid's, unique and close ties to the intelligence community as well as his influence, which was rumored to reach directly into the White House, allowed the team access to information unavailable to private citizens.

Even if Daria convinced Ryker to help her, he'd have to take the mission to Logan Kincaid, the head of the group, for approval. Although the team worked together, they were a loose-knit organization, living in different parts of the country between missions. Kincaid believed in paying his people well, in allowing them partial ownership in the Shey Group, and he preferred the team to rest up between their often dangerous missions. Ryker wondered what Kincaid would think about what Daria was about to tell him.

At a time like this, his sophisticated leader would no doubt fall back on impeccable manners and the most courteous of tones, giving himself time to fully assess the situation. But the polite manners of society hadn't been drilled into Ryker early enough to come automatically. As a child he'd been too busy dodging the slaps of his alcoholic father. In college he'd worked three jobs to pay his way through.

The kind of women who didn't need to say a word for others to recognize that they shopped in the up-scale department stores and breezed through life on Daddy's connections usually had no interest in Ryker, nor he in them—so he hadn't much practice dealing with a lady like Daria Harrington. And while he'd served his country in the military, he'd gravitated toward women with backgrounds similar to his.

Nope, Ms. Daria Harrington certainly wasn't his usual type, but she fascinated him as she tried to withhold her dismay at his messy office. Especially as dust from the spilled materials rose from the floor and caused her to sneeze.

"Sorry."

She took several tissues out of her purse and used one to wipe her almost perfect nose, oh so delicately. With a second tissue, she wiped the dust from the chair before sitting on the edge with her back ramrod stiff. She acted as though slouching or relaxing was a shooting offense.

And for the life of him, he couldn't understand how the woman could worry about dust on her chair after the bombshell she'd thrown at him. But people reacted differently to stress. He still had trouble wrapping his mind around the concept that this woman could really believe she'd killed Harry Levine.

"How did you find me?" he asked.

"Harry's attorney told me to hire you."

The Shey Group had hired Harry's attorney when they'd needed legal counsel. So it wasn't surprising that she'd shown up here.

"Why don't you start at the beginning?" he suggested, working to keep his tone civil.

She replied almost primly. "Six weeks ago, Harry and Fallon, my sister, came to my office for a meeting."

"About?"

"It doesn't matter."

"Let me be the judge of that." At her startled reaction, he added, "Okay?" to soften his statement. He had to remind himself that this woman had probably never been questioned roughly. But he was getting ahead of himself.

"Fallon came to my office at my request. Harry always accompanies her, but never interferes—never interfered—in the business." She'd corrected her tense as if she had trouble remembering or believing that Harry was actually dead. "My sister wanted to open a branch in Tokyo and—"

"What kind of work do you do?" he asked, finding himself more intrigued by the minute. He'd figured her for one of those women who did charity work and spent the rest of the day having their nails done. So much for first impressions. But then, he'd always been better with machines than people.

"We own—I own—Harrington Bouquet."

"The fancy flower shops?" He should have realized sooner. But first she'd bowled him over with her looks and then swept him away with her murder confession.

She nodded. "Fallon was opening new shops faster than I could keep up with the paperwork."

He couldn't imagine this woman hunching over a desk, dealing with paperwork, and realized he'd judged her more like a kid from the poor side of the tracks than a man who had seen his share of the world. Lots of wealthy women worked. He knew that, once he actually stopped to think. And he recalled from a business article in the *Wall Street Journal* that he'd read last year during a trip from Casablanca to Istanbul, Harrington Bouquet was quite the success story.

"You and your sister argued?"

"We disagreed at first, but had come to a compromise. She agreed to stay in New York long enough to help me hire more in-house staff."

"And Harry took no part in this discussion?"

"I don't believe he said a word."

"Okay. What happened next?"

She didn't shift uncomfortably in her chair. If anything, she held every muscle tight, sat perfectly still. "I served them coffee and opened a tin of cookies. They drank the coffee, ate the cookies and then...they died."

Bestselling Author

TAYLOR SMITH

On a cold winter night, someone comes looking for Grace Meade
and the key she holds to a thirty-five-year-old mystery. She is
tortured and killed, and her house is set ablaze. Incredibly,
the prime suspect is her own daughter, Jillian Meade, a woman
wanted in connection with two other murders of women Grace
knew during the war. And FBI Special Agent Alex Cruz has to find
Jillian before her past destroys her for good.

DEADLY GRACE

A "first-rate political thriller."
—*Booklist*

On sale April 2003
wherever paperbacks are sold!

MTS945

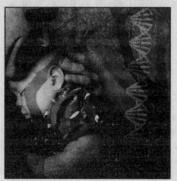
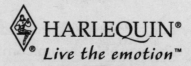

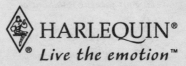